Samuel Laing

A Sporting Quixote

Samuel Laing

A Sporting Quixote

ISBN/EAN: 9783743423145

Manufactured in Europe, USA, Canada, Australia, Japa

Cover: Foto ©Raphael Reischuk / pixelio.de

Manufactured and distributed by brebook publishing software (www.brebook.com)

Samuel Laing

A Sporting Quixote

A SPORTING QUIXOTE

OR,

THE LIFE AND ADVENTURES

OF THE

HON^BLE. AUGUSTUS FITZMUDDLE,

AFTERWARDS EARL OF MUDDLETON.

BY

S. LAING,

AUTHOR OF "MODERN SCIENCE AND MODERN THOUGHT."

IN TWO VOLUMES.
VOL. I.

LONDON: CHAPMAN AND HALL,
LIMITED.
1886,

CHARLES DICKENS AND EVANS
CRYSTAL PALACE PRESS.

PREFACE.

NOVEL READERS, BEWARE!

THOSE who read novels for ingenious plots, stirring incidents, and sensational characters, are warned that nothing of the sort is to be found on these premises; and that, on the contrary, spring-guns are set which may explode unexpectedly, and compel them either to throw down the volume in disgust, or go through the exceedingly disagreeable process which is known as thinking.

Indeed it may be doubted whether this little book deserves the name of a novel at all. Is "Don Quixote" a novel? or "Sartor Resartus"? For those are the models which, more or less consciously, and at a humble distance, the author has endeavoured to follow, rather than the traditional type of the three-volume novel.

The book originated with some sketches of sporting misadventures made to amuse grand-children. The next process was to write short descriptions to illustrate the sketches. Then the idea gradually arose of making the hero a sort of modern Don Quixote, and trying to develop the theme that goodness is better than smartness; and show how a shy, sensitive, awkward youth, spoiled by a silly education, was gradually transformed from a muff into a man, and from a man into a model of a simple-minded, kind-hearted, generous, and honourable specimen of an English gentleman.

And then other ideas came crowding in of trying on this canvas to paint life-like pictures of a number of scenes, experiences, and reflec-tions, which, in the course of a long and busy life, had photographed themselves vividly on the author's brain and memory.

Thus the book came to be that *olla podrida* of

miscellaneous ingredients which the reader will find it. Whether they make a dainty dish fit to set before a king, or a coarse mess, which it requires the "dura messorum ilia," the rigid digestive organs of hungry reapers, to assimilate, is for the reader and not the author to say. No man is a judge in his own case, and least of all is an author in regard to his own production.

All I can say is this, that if I have failed to make judicious readers laugh, and in laughing love, and in laughing and loving think, the work is a failure, and the author will be the first to recommend that it be swept as "rubbish to the void" and forgotten.

CONTENTS.

Part I.

CHAPTER I.

CHAPTER II.

CHAPTER III.

CHAPTER IV.

CHAPTER V.

CHAPTER VI.

CHAPTER VII.

CHAPTER VIII.

CHAPTER IX.

CHAPTER X.

CHAPTER XI.

CHAPTER XII.

CHAPTER XIII.

A MODERN QUIXOTE.

CHAPTER I.

MRS. HUNTER'S LITTLE GAME—FITZMUDDLE'S PARENTAGE AND EDUCATION.

"'THE Fitzmuddles are all fools,' so they say in Sillyshire, and they ought to know a fool in Sillyshire when they see one, for if report speaks true there are plenty of them in that county."

"But, Julia, they are a good family, and they are fortunate fools. When the old Earl of Muddleton died he had more than half ruined himself on the turf; but the present Earl had not succeeded to the title for twelve months when coal and iron were found on the estate, and pits sunk, and Muddleton became quite a large manu-

facturing town, and now the rent-roll is put at
not less than £30,000 a year. And the second
brother, John—the one in the Guards, you know—
is well provided for by that rich old uncle who
was governor of so many colonies ; and now poor
dear Lady Augusta is dead, and Augustus has
come in for her whole property, which I have
reason to know brings in £6,000 a year, all well
invested."

Thus said Mrs. Hunter to her daughter Julia,
as they were sitting over their cup of afternoon
tea in the little drawing-room of their little house
in Mayfair.

She was a well-got-up, fashionable-looking
widow approaching fifty years of age, of considerable pretensions but slender means, and her
only daughter, Miss Julia Hunter, was a fac-
simile of her mother, with the advantage of being
some twenty-five years younger.   With this
advantage she was still a fine, showy girl, and
might even, when carefully made up and seen
by candle-light, pass for a beauty. But five
London seasons will tell their tale, and the bloom

of a youthful cheek is sorely tried by crowded assemblies, late balls, and glaring gas; while the delicate curves of a mobile mouth are apt to get set, and drawn down at the corners, by the anxieties and heartaches incidental to disappointed hopes, and the feeling that your stock is going steadily down in the matrimonial market. Hence Miss Julia's radiant smiles haunted you with a suspicion that they were just the least bit artificial; and to whisper a secret known only to her and her maid, there were other more material matters than smiles, in which Art may have been called in to assist Nature.

But to return to our dialogue. The fair Julia said with a sigh: "But, mamma, he is not a common fool, he is an exceptional fool."

"Don't talk nonsense, Julia," said her mother somewhat sharply. "If a man who is an Honourable and has £6,000 a year has not a right to be a fool, I don't know who has; and I tell you what, Julia, the real fool is the girl who, if she has a chance of catching him, lets him slip through her fingers."

"But, mamma," pleaded Julia, "it is really not my fault. I have tried my very best, but he is so queer, and shy, and awkward, that if I make up to him he gets frightened ; and if I don't, he slips off to some corner, and I see no more of him ; and you must not suppose that there are not other mothers in the world, and other girls too, who keep a sharp look-out to catch him if they could but see a chance. And he goes to so few parties I seldom meet him, and in short I feel that I have really no chance in London, and unless Providence locked us up together in some country house I really don't see what hope there is for me."

"Julia," said Mrs. Hunter, "more impossible things have happened. Now listen to me. Our maid Clara has been keeping company with his footman, and she has found out that his master is going off to Scotland, to some out-of-the-way place in the Highlands in the island of Mull; and he is going alone, for he does not want to have any one with him to laugh at him in his first essay at shooting grouse. Now

you and I both want a change of air, and what
more natural than that we should take a tour in
the Highlands; and, if so, why should we not
happen to meet him on the pier at Oban, and
go in the same steamer to Tobermory, or whatever is the horrid name of the place the Mull
steamer calls at? And as we were so intimate
with his poor aunt, and he has known us so
long, he cannot in common politeness avoid
asking us to pay him a visit at his lodge, and
perhaps stop a week with him; and then, Julia,
I shall have brought you to the post and dropped
the flag, and it is for you to make the running."

"You are a wonderful woman, mother dear,"
said Julia, and she warmed up on the idea so
much that she suggested whether they might
not waylay him at Euston, and get into the
same carriage. But "No," said her sager
mother, "we should frighten him so that he
would get out at Rugby, or get into one of
those horrid smoking carriages, which seem to
have been invented for the express purpose of
preventing girls from getting acquainted with

eligibles in railway trains. And, Julia, there is one consideration which is quite conclusive— girls who are in their fifth London season don't look their best in the gray morning light, after travelling all night on the railway; and you can't afford to throw any chances away. So we will just go down the day before and meet him at Oban."

Julia could not but see the wisdom of this and assent to it; so, when they had ascertained the exact day Fitzmuddle was to start, they packed up their belongings, and started the day before by the Scotch mail for Oban.

While they are travelling northwards by the train we will take the opportunity of describing the Honourable Augustus Fitzmuddle a little more in detail.

He was, as may be gathered from Mrs. Hunter's remarks, the third and youngest son of the late Earl of Muddleton.

Now, the late Earl had a sister, the Honourable Lady Augusta Fitzmuddle, whose career in a former generation had been not altogether unlike that of Miss Julia Hunter. She had struggled, and fought, and flirted through a great many London seasons, and all without result, for those were the days when the Earl was impecunious, and the daughters of the noble house were slenderly provided for. And Lady Augusta was not a beauty, very far from it. She had a foolish face, with gooseberry eyes, and a clumsy figure, which, as years advanced, threatened to develop into formidable dimensions. But at length the right man came in the shape, not of a fairy prince, but of a pursy little stockbroker, Muggins by name, whom she met one winter when she went with old Lady Muddleton to Brighton. Now Muggins was not only pursy in person, but pursy in the sense of having a heavy purse, for he had made a deal of money on the Stock Exchange; and when he went down to Brighton, and drove his open phaeton along the King's Road, with a pair of high-stepping horses in the most resplendent harness, and with a servant behind in the most gorgeous of liveries, and with his hat on one side, and his well-oiled, glossy

curls, and his eyeglass, and multitudinous rings
and lockets, and massive gold chain, Mr.
Manasseh Muggins, let me tell you, looked, in
spite of his crooked nose and yellow complexion,
what in the vernacular of the present day is
called " no end of a swell." Now, Mr. Muggins,
as he grew rich, felt stirrings of ambition in him,
and his great ambition was to ally himself to
the British aristocracy. So he met Lady Augusta
one evening at a party, and, although he did
not exactly fall in love at first sight, his fancy
conjured up to him as he lay awake that
night, not the charms of his *innamorata*, but
the vision of a paragraph in the *Morning
Post*, announcing how Mr. Muggins and Lady
Augusta Muggins had arrived from their
residence in Portland Place at the Bedford Hotel,
Brighton, and he thought it read well; and
next morning he saw it again in his mind's
eye and thought it read better; and as he sat
in his gorgeous dressing-gown and smoked his
cigar after breakfast, he dreamed dreams and
saw visions. He saw the name of Muggins as

presented at a levée by the Right Honourable the Earl of Muddleton, and Lady Augusta Muggins at a Drawing-room on her marriage to Manasseh Muggins, Esq., and other infinite glories. So being a prompt, energetic man of business, he set to work at once to lay siege to the heart of the fair Augusta.

The noble lady and her noble relatives at first had scruples as to mixing the blue blood of all the Fitzmuddles with the more terrestrial fluid which gave warmth and expression to the Semitic features of the plebeian Muggins. But the lady reflected that in the words of the Scotch song,

I'm noo mair than twenty, my time is but sma',

and that although her blood might be blue, the tip of her nose was beginning to assume just a *soupçon* of that primary colour which in the rainbow or spectrum is farthest removed from blue.

And the noble Earl, her brother, happened to be just then in one of his worst fits of impecuniosity, for had not an outsider defeated by a head his horse who was such a red-hot favourite for the Derby? So as Muggins was excessively liberal in the matter of settlements and money, he pocketed his pride and received him as a man and a brother.

Thus the Muggins suit prospered, and the visions which his eye "in a fine frenzy rolling," had conjured up in the night watches, were converted into positive palpable realities, and remain recorded for future generations in the columns of the *Morning Post.*

Years rolled by and Manasseh grew richer and richer, but also, alas! fatter and fatter, and his head seemed to subside quite between his shoulders; and thus having dined one evening at a City feast, not wisely but too well, he had an apoplectic fit and was gathered to his fathers, and, let us hope, taken to the bosom of father Abraham, and not left out in the cold, or rather in the hot, on the wrong side of that great gulf. I am sure he did not deserve to be, for with all his little vanities and foibles, he was at bottom a worthy, kind-hearted man, and made a good husband to Lady Augusta; and one good deed at least is to be recorded to his credit, for having no children, he left all his fortune to his widow, and thus indirectly supplied the ways and means which enabled our hero to take his shooting place in Mull, and thus caused this true and veracious history to be written.

The transfer of this £150,000 worth of good solid securities into the name of Augustus Fitzmuddle, came about as follows:

Lady Augusta found herself lonely after her husband's death, and though she lavished stores of affection on a Persian cat, and a pug, Topsy, who had the merit of being about the ugliest pug in creation, she also had a heart, though it might be a flabby one, somewhere in the recesses of her ample bosom, and she longed for human love and sympathy. Then she bethought herself that there was a little Augustus, who was her godson and had been named after her, and she saw the face of a pretty, delicate little boy, with long, fair, curly hair, who had come shyly up to her, and called her "dear aunt," when she was last at Muddleton—though the "dear," I am afraid, was somewhat associated with a present she had brought him of a splendid box of chocolate bonbons. And she thought that to have such a pet as this always with her, might be better, if that were possible, than even the company of her dear delightful Topsy and that charming cat.

So she entered into negotiations with the Earl, and it was duly stipulated between the high contracting parties that little Augustus should go and live with her, and be her adopted son, and inherit her fortune.

Thus little Augustus came into the hands of—well, not quite the fattest—but assuredly about the most foolish woman in England, for as she waxed old she developed quite a phenomenal amount of the proverbial Fitzmuddle foolishness. Her one idea of his education was to treat him exactly as she treated her favourite pug, and as Topsy was never taken out without a ribbon round his neck and a footman to lead him, so Augustus was never allowed to venture out of the house without a nurse at his heels, and arrayed in the most gorgeous attire. For Lady Augusta had been bitten by the mania for æstheticism, and had a great idea of making her boy look picturesque, as if he had stepped out of a Vandyke canvas. So she arrayed him in the most sumptuous velvets, and slashed satin sleeves, and bows of ribbons stuck on his hat and shoulders, and a prodigious rose-coloured sash round his poor little waist, so that every one turned to look at him, and the nursemaids in the park stopped their perambulators and said, "What a sweet pretty child, and how becomingly he is dressed!" while the rough little boys put out their tongues and said, "Oh, my eye, Bill, just look at that little guy."

As he grew bigger the same system prevailed, for she grew fonder of the boy every day, and her greater fondness translated itself into the form of greater foolishness.

She could not bear the thought of her little darling going to a public school among a lot of rough boys, to get cuffed and knocked about, and perhaps, if he went to Eton or Harrow, made to fetch and carry, and toast his master's bread or slice of bacon. And as an excuse to herself for keeping him at home she developed an idea that the boy's health was delicate; an idea which I am sorry to say that celebrated London physician, Dr. Manyfee, did not combat with all the decision that might have been required by a strict regard for medical science, for, you see, Lady Augusta's fees for professional visits to herself and her boy did not certainly average less than two guineas a week, and there are fifty-two weeks in the year, and one hundred guineas a year for prescribing harmless pills to an old lady, and shaking his head and looking wise when her nephew's health was mentioned, was not to be despised even by the greatest of fashionable M.D.'s.

So poor Augustus was kept at home, and had private tutors, most decorous, gentleman-like, feeble-minded men, who had been to the University and just struggled through into honours; and a smooth, subservient French tutor, full of grins and shrugs and grimaces, who gave out that he was an exiled nobleman; and a spectacled German—but he was soon dismissed, for he took his duties too much in earnest, and Augustus had a headache one day, attributable to his efforts to find the key-note at the end, to a sentence which began in the middle of one page and ran overleaf into the middle of the next one; and drawing-masters who had failed to get their productions into the Academy; and music-masters who were not quite good enough to get a place in an orchestra.

Now as far as positive instruction goes, I do not know that he was much the worse for it, and he probably learned more about things in general, than an average Eton boy who had been spending six years of his life in grinding out Latin hexameters and learning just as much Greek as it took him six months to forget.

But he missed, poor boy, learning a great deal that is more valuable than Latin hexameters, and which ordinary boys learn at public schools —the art of living with one's fellows, and giving

and taking in the rough discipline of scholastic
life, which is of such inestimable advantage for
future manhood.

Least of all can a boy, who is naturally of
a shy and reserved temperament, afford to dis-
pense with this discipline. Shyness is a quality
which grows upon one by leading a solitary life.
It is a very curious quality. Some are born with
a naturally genial and expansive nature which
overflows of itself in talk, and delights in the
society of others. Others, and they the majority,
are made of the common average clay of human
nature, and are neither particularly expansive
nor particularly sensitive, but very much what
circumstances and surroundings mould them into.
But there are a few, and they often of the
finer and more delicate clays, who are born
with a sort of instinctive shyness which it is
extremely difficult to shake off. I have known
a man who had gone through many experiences
and who was genial, intelligent, and brave as
a lion, and yet to his dying day, if he saw
an acquaintance in the street, felt an instinct

prompting him to turn round a corner and pass unseen.

And with boys naturally shy, and in whom shyness has been increased by living much alone, this feeling is apt to assume a morbid acuteness which is quite unintelligible to commonplace natures. I once knew a boy who, having gone for his holidays on a visit to an uncle, received a letter from his father, bidding him ask his uncle to order for him a suit of clothes and an extra pair of trousers. The poor boy was shy and nervous, and got so confused that when he delivered the message he made it "a pair of clothes and a suit of trousers." His uncle laughed, and asked him if he had got two bodies and only one leg, and the boy felt more miserable at having committed such a stupid blunder than most boys would have done if they had been detected in telling a lie or robbing an orchard. And yet that boy lived to be a man who, like Tennyson's Ulysses, might say:

" Much have I seen and known,
   Cities of men and climates, councils, governments,"

and if not exactly "honoured of them all," he might fairly claim to have held his own with most of them.

For a certain fund of shyness, or, if you like to call it, sensitiveness and natural modesty, is a far better foundation to build upon than the fluency and over-confidence which, in nine cases out of ten, spring from coarseness of fibre and want of imagination to realise what others may be thinking of you.

This is specially seen in the House of Commons, where no one ever rises to distinction who has the fatal gift of fluency. Real orators always speak with a great amount of effort, amounting in many cases to hesitation and embarrassment. Lord Beaconsfield never was a fluent speaker, and his polished, stinging sarcasms, and sharp, incisive epigrams, owed a great deal of their effect to the hesitating speech, from which they came suddenly twanging forth like arrows from the bow of an Apollo.

John Bright, the greatest natural orator of modern times, is by no means a fluent speaker until he is fairly roused, and has warmed up upon his subject.

Gladstone may be considered an exception. It is not really so, for his marvellous power as an orator is mainly owing to the intense white heat of conviction into which he has the gift of working himself up in the arena of parliamentary conflict, or on a platform addressing an excited multitude. Watch him in a great speech, and you will see whether he speaks easily or not. You will see the working of the brain within reflected in the working of the brow, and in every vehement gesture and impassioned accent. Take this fervour away, and set him down calmly in his study to write a book or an article, and you will see the demigod subside into a very ordinary mortal, who writes long involved sentences, and buries his leading ideas and central facts under such a mass of side issues and irrelevant topics, that all sense of proportion is lost, and the picture becomes a blurred and nebulous haze. So true is it that the principle of the " Conservation of Energy " applies to the spiritual as well as to the material world, and that whether it be a speech, a poem, a novel, or a picture, the effect produced will be that of the amount of experience and observation, and above all of feeling, emotion, and effort, that has been put into it.

To return from these somewhat high-soaring speculations to the case of our young Augustus, it will not be surprising if the effect of such an education as his aunt gave him on a naturally shy and sensitive disposition was to exaggerate these qualities into a sort of n-th power, or superlative degree, of shyness and sensitiveness. As he grew older he shrank more and more from intercourse with strangers, and shut himself up more and more in a world of his own, consisting mainly of day-dreams.

Among these day-dreams a subject which you would hardly have expected occupied a considerable space—that of sport.

It came about as follows:

Lady Augusta's eminently respectable establishment had at its head an eminently respectable butler, John Tompkins by name. In fact, respectable is not the word for it: he was so superlatively respectable, so exceptionally grave and decorous in demeanour, that "Reverend" would have been the fitter appellation. In a shovel-hat and apron he would have made a very passable bishop; and this much is certain, that, if invested with archidiaconal functions, he would have made almost as good an archdeacon as that dear Dr. Grantly, whom we have never ceased to love since that little Grace Crawley twisted the shrewd old man of the world round her little finger, and Mrs. Grantly told him, when his head was laid on the conjugal pillow, that "she knew how it would be, he was so soft-hearted."

Such was Tompkins to the outward eye; but, alas! in this world it is not always safe to judge by appearances. The real man remains safely ensconced behind his outer lineaments, and rarely exhibits a glimpse of his true self to a casual observer. I have taken many a lady down to dinner, and tried to pump up conversation about the opera and the weather, and thought her hopelessly commonplace, and she has doubtless returned the compliment, and thought me the same, while perhaps all the time she was struggling with suppressed emotion, or bursting with information, or keenly desirous of imparting or receiving knowledge upon high questions of morality or religion. But I was shy, and she was reserved, and we parted without having the least glimmering of a suspicion of what, in either case, might lie hid beneath the frigid surface of dinner-party conventionality.

Thus, in our archidiaconal butler's case, what really lay hid was a soul devoted to sport—a soul which might have been a sort of compound of Assheton Smith and Admiral Rous rolled into one. Unbounded was his admiration of the doings of Dick Christian and the many heroes whose fame is recorded in the description of brilliant runs across Leicestershire in the old *Sporting Magazine;* and specially deep his erudition in pedigrees, and races, and all matters of turf lore. His great delight was on Sunday afternoons, after having gone to church in the morning with an enormous prayer-book, as beseemed his respectability of place and demeanour, to ensconce himself in his pantry with the *Field* and *Bell's Life*, and read; and as he read, meditate profoundly on the state of the odds and the chances of favourites. And then he would go down to the Upper Servants' Club, and deliver oracular sentences, or, it may be, shake his head and look wise—wiser even than Lord Burleigh—and hint that "he knowed what he knowed," and that for all that the baron's horse was such a red-hot favourite, he should not wonder if there were a screw loose somewhere.

His tips and selections of winners of great stakes were something wonderful, though some did whisper behind his back that they were always a day behind the fair, and only assumed precise and definite shape after the telegraph wires had flashed the news to sporting clubs, when oracular utterances and wise shakes of the head were exchanged for, "I told you so; I always knowed it was sure to come off." However, these were probably detractors envious of his fame, or, if they spoke the truth, it only speaks for Tompkins' superior wisdom, who, without reading Mark Twain, had independently worked out for himself the sage aphorism of "never prophesying unless you know."

Now, the sage Tompkins and young Master Augustus were great cronies, for the boy was always pleasant and affable with the servants, and was a favourite with them. So Tompkins used occasionally to smuggle him into his pantry, and let him read the *Field* and *Bell's Life*, and indoctrinate him with sporting lore. And the boy got so keen about it that he used to save up his pocket-money and invest in old sporting magazines, and read with intense interest of the glorious doings of former days, and think the height of human ambition would be to have been recorded by Nimrod as one of the "hard riders of England."

Often did he stand in imagination at the last fence when the Squire and Captain Ross were fighting out that grand steeplechase, across four miles of hunting country in Leicestershire, so different from the steeplechases of these degenerate days, when second-class racehorses are running to win or lose the odds for professional bookmakers, over made-up fences; and loudly did he swell the cry of " Now Clinker, now Clasher," as the colours, first of one, then of the other, flashed in the van.

And many a Derby did he see run in his mind's eye, as when [Cadland and The Colonel ran their memorable dead heat, and, when about to mount for the decider, Bill Scott stood anxious and nervous beside his mount, while Jem Robinson stood sucking an orange, as cool as a cucumber ; and how Jem just slipped his opponent by half-a-length in coming round Tottenham Corner, and retained the advantage to the end, just landing Cadland the winner.

Or he saw the mighty Flying Dutchman, mightiest of modern steeds, floundering in the dirt, and all but beaten by a despised outsider whom he could have distanced on sound ground ;

from which the sage Tompkins impressed on him the inference, "Always to lay agin the favourite if the ground was deep."

Or he saw the four white legs of Teddington flashing in front all the way down the hill from the Corner, and his jockey turning half-round opposite to the Stand, to see what had become of the field, who were toiling hopelessly after him.

These and many another vision of rattling runs and glorious finishes, and marvellous exploits with rod and gun, rose before young Fitzmuddle's mind, as he sat listening to Tompkins' lore, or poring over sporting magazines, in the butler's pantry in the house in Grosvenor Street; for solitary boys, and for the matter of that solitary men, will "dream dreams and see visions," and build castles in the air, and live in a sort of fairy-land of their own creation. And the less they talk the more they think, while with ordinary mortals the process is reversed, and talking is to a great extent a substitute for thinking.

However, Fitzmuddle's sporting aspirations were destined to remain in this cloud region of airy visions, until he reached the mature age of twenty-five, when Lady Augusta, who had been for some years ailing, caught an attack of bronchitis during a spell of cold east wind in May, which carried her off, and she was gathered to her fathers, poor, kind-hearted, foolish old soul, and buried in due state in Muddleton Churchyard in the tomb of all the Fitzmuddles.

When the funeral was over and the will was read, Augustus found himself the sole heir, with the exception of a few legacies to old servants and a provision for the last surviving pug and Persian cat, and thus came into a free and unencumbered income, which was rather over than under £6,000 a year.

He immediately determined to go in for sport, and took counsel accordingly with Tompkins. That worthy had been so well provided for by the will, as also Maria, the cook, that they determined to give up service and unite their fortunes, combining business with pleasure by investing in a small house at Newmarket, and letting lodgings during the races.

Before leaving, however, Tompkins placed his vast store of experience at the service of his young master, and they studied together the advertising columns of the *Field*. The first question was where to go for the next hunting season.

"Belton, of course," said Tompkins; "it's the head-quarters, and the only place fit for a gentleman of fortune to hunt from."

Perhaps this advice was not quite in accordance with Tompkins' usual wisdom, for Belton is not exactly the place for a novice to go to who has all his hunting experiences to learn. But Fitzmuddle had ridden over so many wide brooks and tremendous oxers in fancy, that this objection did not strike him; and the difference between theory and practice is one which can only be appreciated by actual experiment. Accordingly, seeing an advertisement of a snug bachelor's box, with ample stabling, within a mile of Belton, he wrote and took it.

The question of forming a stud remained, and here Fitzmuddle showed a considerable amount of native sagacity, for he took what, under the circumstances, was probably the best course he could have adopted. His eye caught an advertisement from Lord Hardman, the celebrated M.F.H., who was giving up hunting owing to ill-health, strongly recommending his stud groom, who had been with him for twelve years, understood the care of hunters thoroughly, and was a steady, honest, and respectable man.

Fitzmuddle answered this advertisement, which in due course brought to Grosvenor Street Mr. Martingale, a man of about forty, whose appearance corresponded very well with Lord Hardman's description. Without being slangy or ultra-horsey, there was about him that indescribable something which bespeaks familiarity with horses. He was civil, nicely spoken, and had a clear eye, and an open and honest clean-shaven face.

Fitzmuddle liked his looks, and without fencing or circumlocution, told him exactly how he stood. That he knew nothing about horses himself, and must be, for a pretty long time to come, at the mercy of his stud groom. If Martingale cheated

him, he should be sure to find him out in the
long run; but if he was honest and straightforward, and acted for his master's interests, he
would find him a liberal master, and would have
a good situation for life, if he chose to keep it.
And he concluded by throwing himself on Martingale's honour, and saying he thought he had
an honest face, and he preferred trusting him,
as between man and man, to attempting to interfere with him in matters he did not understand;
and, therefore, he would give him a limit, and
leave him to buy a stud of four hunters and a
hack to begin with, and take them down to Belton,
and get them into good hunting condition for the
opening meet on the 1st November.

Some may think that in acting thus Fitzmuddle showed softness; but I say, on the contrary, he showed great worldly wisdom; for in
a long experience of life I have always found
that nothing gives you such a hold over a man
as assuming that he is a gentleman. Very few
men like to break away from this assumption, and
do mean, dishonourable things, which show that

they are not gentlemen, but swindlers; while, if you show that you distrust them, and set your wits against theirs, they will accept the challenge without scruple; and if, as is probable, if the matter relates to business or horse-flesh, they are sharper than you, they will probably get the best of the encounter.

Be this as it may, the experiment answered perfectly in the present case, for although I could not swear that Martingale may not have taken an occasional tip in the purchase of a horse, or commission from a large horse-dealer, just to keep up the rights and dignity of his position, yet on the whole he was an honest and faithful servant, and got together a very fair stud, as we shall see hereafter, at fair prices, and had them all in capital condition at Reynard Lodge at the beginning of the season.

And the appeal to his honour, and the way in which Fitzmuddle trusted him, gave him really a sincere liking for his new master, and he spared no pains in turning him out properly, and giving him instruction in the art of riding to hounds.

The hunting question thus satisfactorily settled, Fitzmuddle and Tompkins bent their mighty minds to that of selecting shooting quarters in Scotland. After reading innumerable advertisements and agents' lists, they settled on the following:

"Splendid Highland sporting to be let for the season, in the romantic island of Mull.

"The lodge, which is elegantly furnished, and contains two sitting-rooms, six bedrooms, and all suitable offices, is beautifully situated on the shore of one of the finest sea-lochs in the West Highlands. The shootings extend over 20,000 acres, abounding with grouse, black game, wild duck and snipe, and deer are constantly on the ground, as it adjoins the celebrated forest of Ben More. There is a splendid salmon river, and a loch noted for the abundance and fineness of its trout. A kennel of first-rate setters will be left. Bag limited to 800 brace of grouse, 100 brace of black game, and 10 stags."

The advertisement was not more mendacious than such things generally are. There really was a lodge, and a river, and a loch, and although the limit was scarcely necessary, seeing that the grouse would probably limit themselves to about 200 or 250 brace to two fair guns; and the chance of a stag to four or five chances in the season, if you happened to be on good terms with the shepherd, and he sent you word overnight if a stag happened to cross the march; and the salmon river, though fairly good after a spate, presented in ordinary weather about as good a chance as if you threw your fly on the pavement of Regent Street; still, on the whole, I doubt if Fitzmuddle could have done much better than by taking Foulis Lodge, with its splendid shootings and fishings, for his first season's essay in the way of Highland sport.

Thus it came to pass that on the evening after Mrs. Hunter and the fair Julia had gone to Oban, Fitzmuddle found himself ensconced, with all his traps and a battery of newly purchased guns, in a corner seat of a smoking carriage in the Scotch mail, and next day duly delivered on board the steamer for Mull.

Great was the mutual surprise when on going aft, the first faces he encountered were those of Mrs. Hunter and her daughter.

"Good gracious, Mr. Fitzmuddle," said the widow, "who would have thought of meeting you here? What a pleasant surprise! What has brought you here? Are you going to stay in these parts?"

"Oh," said Fitzmuddle, "I have taken a shooting place in Mull and am going down to it. And you, Mrs. Hunter, to what am I indebted for the pleasure of meeting you and Miss Hunter on board the Mull steamer?"

"Why, you see, Mr. Fitzmuddle," replied the lady, "my daughter and I both wanted a change of air after the dissipations of a London season, and as one of our remote progenitors on the female side was said to have come from a place called Tobermory in these regions, we thought we would just run down and see what it was like, and, if it suited, take a lodging there for a couple of weeks or so."

Fitzmuddle was of course astonished and

delighted, or what was the same thing, professed to be so ; and in common civility could not help hoping that they would run over to his lodge for a day or two, and accept such hospitality as he could offer, if they did not mind putting up with rough Highland fare.

You may be sure the invitation was accepted, and that Julia said "it would be so awfully nice and so extremely delightful."

CHAPTER II.

ACCORDINGLY Fitzmuddle was fixed for a visit from the two ladies, not without some inward trepidation; but he put a bold face on it, and named an early day, partly to get it over quickly, and partly so as not to interfere with his shooting, which would not begin for a few days, as he had run down before the 12th of August to see the place and its surroundings, and practise a few shots at sea-birds, to get his hand in before attempting grouse.

So he got carpet-seats up from the cabin for the ladies, and they sat together amicably on the upper deck, admiring the scenery. I have seen a good many fine bits of scenery in my time, but I do not think I have ever come

across anything to beat the sail across the Sound
of Oban on a fine afternoon such as this was,
when you come out of the harbour of Oban,
and see the wide expanse of sea, looking like
a great, calm lake, walled in behind you by
Ben Cruachan, and the whole range of Argyleshire mountains stretching northwards by Loch
Etive and Appin, up to Glencoe ; and in
front of you the great purple masses of the
Morvern Hills on the one hand, and the equally
bold masses of Ben More and the mountains of
Mull on the other ; with green Lismore on the
right, and a hundred little islands of trap rock
just showing their fantastic shapes above the
water. No wonder that, as they watched the
ripple from the steamer's wake spreading over
the calm surface, distorting the reflections in the
azure mirror, and sending a thousand lights
dancing and glimmering, they felt quite sentimental, and Julia, who had carefully provided
herself with a copy of Scott's " Lord of the Isles,"
quoted from it, and contrasted their situation
with that of Bruce's storm-tossed bark, tacking

to and fro the livelong day against a screaming north-wester between Ardtornish and the mainland, and when the shades of evening closed in, and the gusts tore ever more furiously down the narrow Sound, compelled to put in, and land in the very lion's mouth at the castle of the Lord of Lorne.

But before they reached the old Castle of Ardtornish, they had an experience of the sudden changes of the weather on these land-locked seas girt in by lofty mountains, for a great black cloud rose behind them from the south-east, and blotted out Ben Cruachan and his Argyleshire brother giants, and rolling rapidly on, obscured the whole eastern sky, leaving nothing but a faint, sickly gleam of the bright day out to the west, which set off by contrast the dark, leaden-coloured gloom that settled down over the hills of Morvern and of Mull. Every moment this became darker and darker, until the whole sky seemed to be covered with an inky pall, through which the blue-black mountains were seen dimly in a lurid light, while a still blacker wall of cloud came rolling up behind, fringed below by a line of white, where the sea hissed and writhed as the blast and torrent of rain advanced swiftly and steadily along it, like a remorseless foe in pursuit of the solitary steamer. Then, just as the blast struck her, and the raging rain came pouring down, there was a flash of lightning so bright that it dazzled the eye for a second, and seemed to go through and through your whole body; and then, in another second, a peal of thunder, so loud that it seemed as if the whole heavens had been split open by the flash, and were tumbling in headlong ruin upon the devoted steamer. And then for half-an-hour, more flashes, and more thunder, and more rushing torrents of rain, until, as they approached Tobermory, the storm rolled westwards, and the thunder died away in distant mutterings, as if the spirits of Ossian's heroes were retreating, grumbling and dissatisfied, to the recesses of their native mountains.

At the first flash, Julia uttered a scream, for once real and not affected, and retreated with her mother to the protection of the cabin. But

Fitzmuddle stood it out under the shelter of the funnel, and although the rain streamed from his waterproof, and well-nigh battered his hat into a shapeless mass, he thoroughly enjoyed it, for it roused all the latent poetry which most men have in their nature, though for the most part they are unconscious of it, and if accused of being poetical, would deny the soft imputation.

At length the storm ceased, and they landed at Tobermory, where Fitzmuddle, who had telegraphed in advance, had a trap waiting to drive him twelve miles on to his lodge. So he took leave of Mrs. and Miss Hunter, repeating the invitation to them to drive over the next day but one, if they had nothing better to do, and spend a day or two with him.

On the second day the ladies drove over from Tobermory and duly appeared at the lodge, where Fitzmuddle was waiting to receive them. They were of course enchanted with everything, and pronounced the place "too awfully charming." As it was a fine evening Fitzmuddle proposed a stroll down to the side of the loch, to pass the time before dinner, and on arriving there they found a fishing-boat just landing at the small stone pier. It was manned by two hairy giants in oil-skins, and had on board a wonderful haul of halibut, big cod, skate, and haddocks.

Julia conceived a bright idea, and whispered to her mother: " Do let us make a party to go fishing to-morrow, and if you should chance to have a headache when the time comes, I will do my best to entertain Mr. Fitzmuddle." Mrs. Hunter immediately developed a great interest in the result of the deep-sea fishing, and inquired where they had caught so many fine fish, and whether there would be a chance of their catching any if they hired the boat and went out the first fine day.

She was assured that they had only to go about three miles outside the Butt of Mull and set a long line, and they would be sure to catch a lot of large fish, while they could pull up any number of small cod and haddocks with hand lines.

Fitzmuddle thought it would be good fun, and at any rate better than being shut up all day on dry land with two ladies to entertain, so a bargain was struck, and Rorie and Hamish were to have the boat ready with lines and bait, and be at the pier at ten o'clock next morning, if the day was fine.

The morning came and it was very fine, but unfortunately Mrs. Hunter had got such a head-ache, that it was quite impossible for her to leave the house. Fitzmuddle proposed to put off the expedition till she was better, but she would not hear of it, and declared it would make her miser-able to be so abominably selfish as to have the excursion put off on her account, and that if Mr. Fitzmuddle would promise to take great care of her darling Julia, and bring her safe back, she would entrust her to his care. Fitzmuddle was rather staggered by the proposal, but he reflected that the young lady could hardly proceed to any very desperate extremities in the presence of Rorie and Hamish, and she could certainly not run away with him with nothing but the wide Atlantic around them; and Miss Julia was looking her very best, with such a bright rosy complexion,

so he resigned himself to his fate and walked
down to the pier with her, and gallantly handed
her into the boat, and arranged her cushions and
wrappers.

It was one of those lovely early autumn
days which are sometimes met with in the West
Highlands. The air was deliciously clear, the
sky of a tender blue, with a few white clouds
floating lazily in it, as "still as brooding doves,"
and melting away towards the horizon into a
film of the softest purplish-gray haze. The sea
was like a silver mirror, reflecting the hills in
the still loch, and out towards the broad Atlantic
it was flecked here and there with patches of a
deeper azure, where the shadow of some light
cloud rested on it. It was such a sea and sky
as Brett delights to paint, only of a softer and
tenderer tone of colour than that of his brilliant
Cornish Crags and Channel Islands.

While they were in the loch and sheltered
by the bold promontory of the Butt of Mull, it
was simply delightful, and Miss Julia nestled
up close to Fitzmuddle with a thousand little

silly nothings, hoping that he would take care of her, and bait her hook for her, and not let some horrid, monstrous cod pull her overboard. And Fitzmuddle thought what a beautiful colour she had got in her cheeks, and how much the Highland air had improved her already, and, in short, things were going on just as Mrs. Hunter's maternal heart could have desired, when, alas! alas! a sad change came over the scene.

Two, they say, are company, but three are none. And so it proved in the present instance, for when they rounded the point and came out into the wide Atlantic, an intruder appeared in the person of a "great Atlantic swell." A very great swell indeed — a slow, solemn, majestic swell, whose birthplace had been in a cyclone on the borders of the Gulf Stream, and who had travelled in state across the ocean, to visit the shores of the old world.

He was not a rough or rudely-mannered swell; far from it, for the sea was glassy smooth, and the great undulations rose and fell very

much as if you had been on the downs behind
Brighton, and the three smooth, grassy ridges
you could see between you and the horizon had
begun to heave and swell and roll slowly in.
About half-a-mile off was a barque bound for
Glasgow from Riga, with her topsails clewed
up and flapping in the dead calm. Every time
she sank into the trough between the swells,
she seemed to go down and down until the
tops of her royals disappeared, and it seemed
a fearfully long time before the slender poles
reappeared, and she rose slowly until her hull
seemed suspended in the air on the top of an
enormous wave.

But Fitzmuddle and his fair friend were in
no mood to appreciate the sight, for a heavy
ground swell, in a flat calm, under a hot sun,
is trying even to a seasoned stomach. And Miss
Julia's little affected giggles had long since
ceased, and she lay prostrate in the boat, with
her head over the side. And as for poor Fitzmuddle, though he was as far as possible from
being a Don Juan, Byron's lines might have

been well applied to him, for instead of asking
Julia

> To hear him still beseeching,
> He grew quite inarticulate with——

well, a word with which we will not offend the
delicate ears of our readers, but confine ourselves
to suggesting that it makes a capital rhyme to
"beseeching."

Now there is a curious phenomenon in natural
philosophy, that whereas the prismatic gradation
of colour from red to yellow, and from yellow
to blue, produces a most pleasing effect as seen
in the rainbow, it is by no means so attractive
when exhibited on the face of a sea-sick young
lady; and Fitzmuddle, when in an interval of
his paroxysms he turned his head, thought she
did not look quite so well as when he handed
her on board the boat in the morning.

But worse remained behind. The boatmen,
excited by the promise of a sovereign, turned
the boat round and rowed lustily for the shore.
But the tide had turned against them, and they
made slow progress, and as often happens in

these parts, the day suddenly clouded over, and a soft, fine drizzle began to fall, which soon changed into a soaking rain, and as it fell, it fell on Miss Julia's face, who had lost her hat, and was too woebegone to have energy left to put up an umbrella; and what was left of the roses in her cheeks when she put forth in the morning so full of hopes and spirits, with

> Youth at the helm, and pleasure at the prow,

began to disappear, and trickle down in red rivulets over her yellow cheeks, and one drop of pearly, or rather pearl-powdery white, hung pendant from the tip of her blue nose.

Now, young ladies who peruse these pages, let me solemnly warn you: there is only one sin a woman can commit more heinous than that of painting, and that is, painting and being found out. You may break all the commandments of the Decalogue, and still find some Satanic hero who will love you with all the volcanic ardour inspired by murder and sudden death, and by a breach of the seventh commandment—at least, in Ouida's novels, for in actual life such peccadilloes are apt to lead to more prosaic terminations in the Criminal and Divorce Courts. You may break any amount of æsthetic laws; put angles where there ought to be curves, protuberances where Nature has given them to nothing except dromedaries and Hottentot Venuses; frizzle your hair till it loses all trace of what Huxley considers the most characteristic mark of the white Caucasian race, the Leotrochi, with smooth, wavy locks, and makes your naturally glossy, rippling hair a very tolerable imitation of that of a Feejee islander, or one of those Soumalie boys who dive for rupees from the deck of a P. and O. steamer at Aden. The male sex are very obtuse, and any monstrosity which has been worn for a fortnight by all girls alike, and therefore by a fair average percentage of pretty ones, gets connected by the association of ideas with pretty faces, and becomes first tolerable, and finally acceptable.

But there is one thing that men can't stand,

and that is paint. Why should it be so? Perhaps because it is an obvious imposition. No one is taken in by the dromedary humps, and thinks they have any real existence; or by the frizzly hair, and thinks you have really negro blood in your veins; or that the wasp-like waists are due to anything but severe and systematic tightening of stay-laces. But if a man sees a rosy cheek and coral lips, he can't help having a sort of natural feeling that it would be nice to kiss them, and a shudder of physical disgust comes over him if he thinks that the result of such a proceeding, were he adventurous enough to attempt it, would be felt in his mouth for an hour afterwards in a taste compounded of red-lead and pomatum.

Therefore, oh! fair readers, take warning by Julia's fate and don't paint, or if you do don't get found out.

For it really sealed the fate of this unhappy young lady. When at last they got home, she rushed past her astonished mother, ran up to her room and looked in the glass. The glass told the tale only too clearly. "It's all up," she said, and burst into a flood of tears. Mrs. Hunter tried to console her, and to suggest hope where there was no hope. But she argued faintly, for it was against her own conviction, and she soon gave in, and agreed with her daughter that it was useless to waste more time and money in the pursuit of this particular Honourable and his £6,000 a year. So the carriage was ordered from Tobermory. Dear Julia was too much upset to come down to breakfast next morning, her mother too affectionate and solicitous not to sit with her daughter upstairs, and at two o'clock they drove away with a shower of thanks and compliments, and regrets that unavoidable circumstances had curtailed their extremely pleasant visit.

Having thus got rid of Mrs. and Miss Hunter, Fitzmuddle congratulated himself on having escaped, even at the cost of a bout of sea-sickness, from the fascinations of female society. But he had one more experience still to go through; for taking a stroll up the glen after dinner to enjoy his cigar in the cool evening air, he encountered a portentous apparition in the shape of Miss Brownsmith, an elderly and exceedingly strong-minded lady, who was staying at the Free Kirk Manse on a tour of geological exploration. At present her researches were respecting the Glacial period; and if the subject was frigid, no less frigid was her demeanour. She was tall and gaunt, wore spectacles on her prominent nose, and carried in one hand a volume of Geikie's "Great Ice Age," while in the other she wielded a formidable implement, which served the double purpose of an umbrella and a geological hammer. One trait only displayed condescension for the weakness of human, and even of feminine human nature. That was her dress, for her gown was drawn up behind into a prodigious boss, or hummocky protuberance, displaying in front a wide expanse of the very brightest blue-and-yellow striped petticoat, below which might be seen a pair of worsted stockings and stout Balmoral boots.

Perceiving Fitzmuddle, and being intent on

E 2

the search for Glacial phenomena, she thus addressed him :

"Pray, sir, can you tell me if there are any signs of moraine in this glen?"

Geology had, unfortunately, not been one of the subjects included in the range of Fitzmuddle's studies, so he replied :

"More rain, madam? I fear we shall. They tell me it is never two days together without more rain in Mull."

"Sir," she replied scornfully, "my remark had reference to glacial and not to pluvial action; but I presume you were absorbed in contemplation of this very interesting development of a Gneiss formation."

Fitzmuddle, though unversed in the language of geology, knew enough—theoretically, of course, from perusal of yellow-backed novels — of the language of gallantry, to be considerably taken aback by what appeared to him to be such an outspoken reference to her own personal attractions on the part of a respectable middle-aged female. Nevertheless, he speedily recovered himself, and with prompt politeness replied:

"Nice formation; exactly; just so; very nice indeed; and if I may be allowed the remark, admirably set off by a most picturesque costume."

"Sir," said the lady, "your remarks are worthy of your odious and contemptible sex. It is hard to say whether they savour most of ignorance or of impertinence."

And with that she tossed her head on high and stalked majestically up the glen, leaving Fitzmuddle in a state of intense bewilderment to know how he had offended her. For Miss Brownsmith, be it known, was not only great in geology, but great upon woman's rights, and her figure was a familiar one in drawing-room gatherings and upon platforms where strong-minded ladies congregate to declaim upon the emancipation of Woman from the tyranny of that odious monster, Man.

Oh! my shrieking sisters, it is a sin to laugh at you, for you are earnest in what you believe to be a sacred cause, and there really are many things in social arrangements and legislation which bear hardly on the weaker sex.

If centuries of landlord legislation have made the law of England too favourable for the owners, and too unfavourable for the occupiers of land, still longer centuries of the supremacy of male brute force, and latterly of male legislators and judges, have doubtless left their traces in our common law and statute-book, and there are many things in which the weaker half of creation do not get, I will not say protection, but even fair play. It is impossible to read many of the trials in the Divorce Court, or for the right to property or custody of children, without wishing that what is "sauce for goose were sauce for gander," and it makes one's blood boil with indignation to read of some great hulking brute, who has half battered his wife to death, getting off with a less punishment than if he had shot a rabbit, instead of receiving the six dozen, soundly laid on with a cat-o'-nine-tails, which he so richly deserves.

Still, I may be allowed to doubt whether

platform oratory is the best way to obtain redress, even for these admitted evils; and as regards the position of woman generally, I may observe that it has enormously improved with the progress of civilisation, even although it had not the aid of Miss Brownsmith's imposing presence and tremendous oratory.

Just think what was the position of woman in those Palæolithic ages, when glaciers were scattering the boulders which now resounded to the stroke of Miss Brownsmith's hammer.

Captain Fitzroy, in the "Voyage of the *Beagle*," gives a most vivid account of what the life of women is like among the Fuegian savages. He describes how he saw a brutal savage, in a fit of passion with his wife because she had dropped a basket of sea-eggs, for which she had been diving, snatch her baby from her breast, and dash it on the rocks; and how the poor creature had to swallow down the tears which, mixed with melting snow, were pouring down her face, and go out again and dive in the ice-cold sea for more sea-urchins.

Contrast this with the picture of a smart American girl entering a tram-car and claiming the best seat as a matter of right ; while that respectable elderly citizen who sat there jotting up the note of his dealings in Wall Street, and calculating how many hundred dollars he had made or lost by his day's operations, has to squeeze into a corner and make room for her.

Whether the male half of creation gain or lose by the spread of democratic institutions and the progress of civilisation, may possibly admit of argument, but there can be none that the female half are clear gainers, and that there is a sort of regularly *crescendo* scale in their condition from slavery to freedom, from Turkey to America.

Moreover, there is another consideration which has to be weighed before deciding on giving women equal political rights. How much of the tyranny from which they suffer is a question of legislation and how much of fashion ? I should say that at the very least nine-tenths of female suffering is due to strictly preventible causes, and would disappear if the sex had but the strength of mind to assert itself against the decrees of that little "Vehmgericht" of Parisian shop-keepers and man-milliners who make and un-make fashions with such startling rapidity.

Why should that fair girl hobble about on poor cramped toes and deform her pretty little feet with corns and bunions, because some un-known authority has decided that she must wear high-heeled boots? Or why should that other girl strain at her stay-laces, at the risk of sending all the blood to her face, or for want of lung-space to oxygenate it properly, depositing adipose matter in regions where, to say the least, it is not becoming, all because some Parisian milliner wants orders, and bribes some great lady to set the fashion?

Three years ago ladies went about so tightly encased in close-fitting habiliments, that you could not help fearing that if one single lace or hook gave way, the whole structure would collapse and burst like the shell of a chrysalis, revealing the form within

In beauty unadorned, adorned the most.

Now, the tightness is confined to the central region, and all below swells and expands into voluminous excrescences. For this, no Acts of Parliament are responsible. How can we trust you to reform the laws, while you show such abject imbecility in the reform of dress? What says Carlyle: "Do the duty that lies nearest to you, and already your next duty will have become plainer." So say we in this matter of woman's rights. Show a little more sense and taste in wearing what is useful and becoming, and not following every varying caprice of fickle fashion, and you will have emancipated yourselves from nine-tenths of your practical discomforts and disabilities, and advanced your claim for equality of legal and political rights more than by a thousand harangues from a thousand Miss Brownsmiths.

However, if such speculations ever entered Fitzmuddle's mind, which I am inclined to doubt, they vanished with the vanishing form of the lady as she stalked majestically up the glen, "nursing her wrath to keep it warm," and revolving in her mind how she could turn the episode into a telling period in her next speech at the Woman's Rights Society.

But Fitzmuddle finished his cigar and walked down to the lodge to go to bed and dream of shooting grouse, for the morrow was the 12th of August.

CHAPTER III.

THE TWELFTH OF AUGUST—GROUSE AND BLACK GAME.

HAIL, sacred bird, peculiar product and glory of the British Islands! Whether miraculously created from the soil in fullest plumage, or slowly transformed from aboriginal ptarmigan, who fed on lichens growing on the storm-swept rocks rising above the icy sea of the British Archipelago in remotest Glacial periods; in either case, here at any rate is an illustration of the doctrine of final causes, and of one unceasing purpose running through the changes of creation.

For if there were no grouse, how would sessions of the British Parliament ever come to an end? If a blessed time ever arrives, when "the wicked cease from troubling and the weary are at rest," when the drone of interminable harangues and the groans of much-enduring senators no longer resound in the halls of Westminster; when a Warton ceases to block, and a Biggar to count out; when Gladstone's eloquence comes to an end, and ill-mannered young Tories no longer interrupt by jeers; to thee are we indebted, O bird of the bright eye and ruddy plumage! But for thee, why should not the House be still sitting? and why should not that Irish Member who talked it out that Wednesday afternoon, to his own cheek be still talking? There is no apparent reason "in the heaven above, the earth beneath, or the waters under the earth," why he should ever stop, and why that tepid flow of exceedingly diluted milk-and-water oratory should not flow on, "In omne volubilis ævum," until he had exhausted the many millions of possible combinations of amazing adjectives and incoherent interjections in the English language.

But the 12th of August is at hand, and it brings deliverance, thanks to thee, O saviour of suffering statesmen and friend of distracted humanity! thou prophet of the great truth, that if there is a time for speech there is a time also for silence, and that, in presence of the immensities and eternities, the latter may often be of gold while the former is of silver!

On this particular 12th of August, however, Fitzmuddle's mind was not exercised by these high speculations as he breasted the hillside and came out upon the open moor, eager for the fray, and full of youthful excitement. For in his case the nature which had been so long repressed by his surroundings during his aunt's lifetime, was now bursting forth into early bloom, and though he was a man of twenty-five in years, he was in many respects a boy of fifteen in feelings. He had all the boy's keen delight in the mere idea of firing off a real gun at real game, and should he perchance knock over an old cock grouse at thirty yards, his transports would be greater than if, in after life, he had slaughtered a whole hecatomb of pheasants.

Oh, golden days of youth, will you never

return ? Shall I never again tread the elastic heather with an elastic step, and breast the mountain side like a mountain deer, and never again feel intense delight if I hit a difficult shot, and intense disgust if I miss an easy one ? No, to each age are its appointed duties and pleasures, and I must now take my sport soberly, and slacken my step when I come to a steep brae, and go out late and return early, and not grudge the half-hour for lunch, and even spin it out for another ten minutes while I smoke a cigarette. And by-and-by I shall have to sit in my arm-chair and do my shooting by proxy by sons, or as years roll on by grandsons, though I shall always retain a green spot in my memory for the blooming heather, and the sagacious setter, and the whir of the rising covey, and the gallant cock grouse with his crow of defiance as he skims away over the brae ; and having loved these things dearly, I will say with the poet :

'Tis better to have loved and lost,
Than never to have loved at all.

But in the case of Fitzmuddle's earlier experiences I am afraid that these lines ought to
be paraphrased:

> 'Tis better to have shot and missed,
> Than never to have shot at all.

Hold! No, I am wrong; for his very first shot
that morning was a most palpable hit, though
the mark was not precisely what he aimed at.

It happened thus:

Sandy McShot, the head keeper, was one of
those short, squat, broad-built, fiery Celts, who
look for all the world like one of their own shaggy
red Highland bulls.   He had a big head, a great,
coarse-lipped mouth, a wide nose with upturned
nostrils, little blinking bloodshot eyes, and a profusion of carroty red shaggy hair and whiskers.
But he took a great pride in his personal appearance, and nothing would ever induce him to
exchange the picturesque garb of the Gael for
the plebeian trouser or the prosaic knickerbocker.
Picturesque, however, as is the garb of the Highlander as he stands in effigy over a tobacconist's

shop, or struts as proud as a swelling turkey-cock like those

> Grants o' Tullochgorum
> Wi' their pipers playing before them,

yet it has its compensating disadvantages.

The kilt is not exactly the most pleasant costume in which to tread the dusty heather on a sultry day, when every footstep raises a swarm of midges; nor is it that in which a friend could be impartially advised to go on an expedition to destroy a wasps' nest. Still less is it conducive to comfort, if the hairy leg and brawny knee find themselves suddenly assailed by something sharper than the stings of wasps, in the form of a shower of small shot.

This Sandy McShot experienced to his sorrow, for when they had gone a couple of hundred yards across the moor the setter's tail feathered and he began to crawl cautiously, and soon came to a dead stand; seeing which Fitzmuddle hastened up with his gun at full cock, outstepping the slower movements of McShot, when suddenly a fine old cock grouse rose from the heather almost under his feet, and flew across the line on which McShot was advancing.

Fitzmuddle's heart gave a mighty bump against his breast; whether he shut his eyes or not I am not quite sure, but he certainly pulled the trigger and blazed away in the direction of the grouse and McShot.

The report of the gun was followed by an explosive "Cot tamn," which went off like the bursting of a bomb, followed by a series of minor explosions and splutterings, which at the rate of half-a-crown per oath, would have run up a long bill against McShot in any police-court where penalties were enforced for profane swearing.

When the smoke cleared away, that worthy was discovered binding a red pocket-handkerchief tightly about the wounded limb. Fitzmuddle in vain made a thousand apologies, and proffered a liberal application of sovereign remedies. The wrath of McShot was not to be appeased, and when he was helped on to the pony, he rode off home in towering indignation, muttering to himself and vowing that nothing should ever induce him to go out again with a "shentleman who couldna tell a Hielandman's bare leg from a cock grouse."

This vow he kept, and to tell the truth, Fitzmuddle was not sorry for it, for McShot was at best but a sulky fellow, and after this misadventure Fitzmuddle was quite afraid to look him in the face, and greatly preferred to be accompanied by Donald Cameron, the head gillie.

Cameron was the very opposite of McShot both in character and in appearance. He was a fine, tall, strapping young fellow of four-and-twenty, with a frank, honest face, fresh complexion, fair curly hair, and clear blue eyes somewhat deeply set under a massive brow.

He looked the very picture of one of those young Norse giants who may have rowed an oar in Olaf Tryggvesson's famous war galley, the *Long Serpent*, or taken a part in the sword-play when the chance arrow pierced the heart of good King Hakon in the moment of victory on the shore of Strand. Indeed, it is probable that he had Norse blood in his veins, for his mother was a Macleod, and the Macleods, as all know, are descended from the sea rover, Torquil, whose descendants, as Walter Scott tells us in the " Lord of the Isles," swore

By Odin wild, their grandsire's oath.

So in future McShot sulked like Achilles in his tent, and Cameron attended Fitzmuddle in all his expeditions.

The two soon got to be excellent friends, for Fitzmuddle had nothing stiff or stuck-up in his nature, and from the first took that surest road to a Scotchman's heart of shaking hands when they met, which is considered as a sort of symbolic recognition of the essential equality of man and man, apart from the mere accidental differences of money and social rank. And when Fitzmuddle offered him a share of his flask, and a cigar from his own case, he quite won Donald's heart ; and the more so, when he told him, simply and frankly, the story of his youth, and how he knew that he was a muff, and almost threw himself upon Donald's compassion, not to laugh at him, and to teach him how to shoot and fish, and do things that other men did.

Accordingly, Donald was assiduous in giving him all the assistance and advice that his experience suggested, and, having an apt and docile pupil, he really taught him in a surprisingly short time to hit his first grouse, and after two or three weeks' practice he could shoot well enough to hit, perhaps, one easy shot out of three, and one difficult shot out of twenty.

Before he reached this degree of proficiency, however, he met with another misadventure. The 20th of August having arrived, he determined to have a try for a blackcock, encouraged thereto by Donald's assurance that there was no easier shot in the world than young black game, and that he knew of a covey or two just outside the birch wood. Accordingly he sallied forth, armed with a new choke-bore, which the gunmaker had warranted to be unrivalled for penetration and close shooting up to sixty yards, and despatched a boy with the shooting pony, game hampers, and luncheon, to meet him at one o'clock at the lower end of the wood. Fitzmuddle and Donald breasted the hill, and though the day was hot, and the hill steep, they never slackened their pace till they had climbed up through the trees and long heather, and got out on the fringe of the wood, where a few scattered birches, gnarled and twisted by a thousand storms, stood like outposts, to guard the main body of the wood against the assaults of the furious westerly gales.

Here they uncoupled the dogs, and the steady old setter soon came to a point; and as Donald predicted, the young black game sat like stones, and had to be kicked up one after another from the ferns and heather, so that Fitzmuddle got five or six shots of the easiest possible description. One he actually bagged, and would have bagged another had not the choke-bore redeemed its reputation by blowing it into a hundred pieces; for, indeed, the bird was not ten yards off when Fitzmuddle pulled the deadly trigger. However, he felt supremely happy looking at the young cock he had shot, and admiring the black feathers just beginning to streak the gray plumage and distinguish it from the soberer hen. How is it, I wonder, that in the bird creation the laws which regulate the human species are so singularly reversed, and it is the male who struts about in ruffs, and plumes, and peacock eyes, and other gorgeous attire, while the female appears generally to have embraced the Quaker persuasion, and eschewed the worldly vanities of dress? Can it be that in some distant age the advocates of woman's rights had so completely carried the day in the inferior order of creation, as to have secured the undisputed right of selection in matters matrimonial, and obliged the poor male to deck himself in brightest plumage, and attitudinise, and put on all sorts of airs and graces to secure favour? Or is it that the bird calendar has somehow got confused, and they make every year a leap year? Be this as it may, the brightness of plumage and general gorgeousness of appearance are attended both in the human genus and that of birds with this disadvantage, that the more attractive specimens are the most sought after by the wiles of the fowler.

Thus in Fitzmuddle's case, though as luncheon-time approached he had succeeded in bagging two-and-a-half brace of young birds and gray-hens, his ambition, growing with what it fed on, felt unsatisfied unless he could succeed in bringing down one of those grand old black-cocks, with the big bodies and glossy blue-black plumage. So true is it that the capacities of the human soul are quite infinite, and if, as Carlyle says, you were to give a cobbler the universe to himself with oceans of porter to drink, he would forthwith begin to grumble for more universes and more oceans.

However, the old blackcock is a wary bird, and though they saw several they all managed to keep at such a safe distance from the redoubt-able choke-bore, that it must be presumed they took in the *Field* and had read the gunmaker's advertisement. So when one o'clock came they gave up the pursuit, and scrambled down through the wood, stumbling over boulders hidden by the long fern and heather, towards the place where they had trysted the boy and pony to meet them for luncheon. But just before they reached it, it chanced that in crossing a little opening among the birches, Fitzmuddle almost trod on a fine old blackcock who had been taking a midday nap in a cluster of fern. Out bounced the bird, and so astonished Fitzmuddle that he never shot until the blackcock had got some thirty yards off among the thick trees. Then he pulled the trigger, and immediately there arose a loud yell, mingled with indignant snortings, and a noise as of a horse plunging and multitudinous crockery breaking. They rushed on to see what might be the matter, and there stood the boy, or rather danced first on one leg, then on the other, rubbing vehemently those regions which had unluckily been in the direct line of Fitzmuddle's barrel when he pulled trigger at the blackcock.

Justice to the eminent gunmaker compels me

to admit that, as regards penetration, the choke-bore showed itself equal to its reputation, for, although the distance was well on to fifty yards, and the boy's corduroy breeks were of the thickest, the shot stung him up so smartly, that nothing short of a sovereign remedy brought the yells to a termination. But as for close carrying, I am afraid there must have been some slight exaggeration, for how did it happen that two such objects as the hinder regions of both boy and pony had been simultaneously invaded by the same enemy? Fitzmuddle therefore acted wisely in suspending his judgment, for although two of the principal parties to the inquiry, the boy and the pony, emphatically pronounced the experiment quite sufficient, and the result alto-gether unsatisfactory, did not their conclusions savour too much of personal considerations to be accepted as final? Better, therefore, would it be to adjourn the inquiry, and postpone any further investigation till after luncheon.

For this meal they had not long to wait, as it had been already laid out. The pony had resented the unfair attack on his rear by a series of such vehement plunges and kicks, that he loosened the hampers, and sent their contents flying in all directions. The cold grouse once more took wing, and skimmed along the tops of its native heather. The ham and bread of the sober sandwiches, indissolubly united for better or worse by wedding tie, parted company as if they had obtained a decree of dissolution *a vinculo matrimonii* in the Divorce Court, and started off each on a separate tour on its own account. The aristocratic champagne forgot the decorous behaviour due to its distinguished lineage, and, after turning a series of somersaults in the air, like the clown in Hengler's Circus, popped off as if it had been a bottle of plebeian ginger-pop on Hampstead Heath or the sands of Margate. Fragments of plates strewed the grass, reminding one of the fate of many a speculator on the turf or Stock Exchange, who, after a brief run of luck and sudden elevation, finds himself hopelessly broke.

Fitzmuddle gazed ruefully on the scene of

destruction, but with Donald's aid they gathered together the fragments, and if they made but a slender meal, an extra cigar and nip of whisky squared the account, and they retraced their steps to the lodge, talking little, but I make no doubt, thinking the more, and as old Homer says of his Greek heroes, revolving the events of the day "backwards and forwards in the swift mind."

CHAPTER IV.

THE SWEET HIGHLAND GIRL.

A FEW days afterwards, Fitzmuddle thought he would try his hand at the snipe, which were said to be abundant in a bog called Squash-na-dub, which lay across the hill about three miles off, on the path to the upper shepherd's cottage. It was a black, miry sort of place, full of peat hags, with a labyrinth of tortuous passages winding among them, and at intervals expanses of what is known as quaking bog, only to be traversed by stepping carefully from one tuft of the red wiry grass to another, while here and there a spring came out, and spread around it a treacherous dome of emerald green, in which either man or horse treading on it would be surely engulphed.

Fitzmuddle went by himself, partly because, like most young men who have led a solitary life, he liked to be occasionally alone, and partly that having a misgiving that his shooting at such a small mark as a snipe might not be of the first order of excellence, he did not wish to have even the faithful Donald to count his misses. So he gave Donald a holiday, and having received from him much excellent advice as to avoiding the treacherous places, and taking care to shoot before the snipe had begun its zigzag flight, he shouldered his gun and marched off across the hill.

When he reached the bog he found the snipe plentiful, and blazed away with no great result. At last he managed to knock one over, and this so excited him that he went farther and farther into the bog, regardless of the clouds which began to close in, and of the mist which came creeping lower and lower down the mountain side. All at once he found himself enveloped in one of those Scotch mists, which they say were invented for the express purpose of wetting an

Englishman to the skin. And worse than the wetting, the mist so obscured the view, that when he tried to retrace his steps and regain firm land, he soon found that he had hopelessly lost his way. A moss on which you cannot walk in a straight line, and take your bearings by the drift of the wet mist on your cheek, but have to turn and twist at every moment to circumnavigate some peat hag, or avoid pools, is a trying position in a fog even for an experienced mountaineer, and I have known more than one who thought himself a proficient, walk round and round under such circumstances, and find himself at the end of an hour at the exact spot from which he started. No wonder, then, that Fitzmuddle floundered about and got hopelessly bewildered. At last he saw something which looked through the driving mist like a firm bank, and he struggled towards it. But he forgot Donald's warning as to the green places, and rushing across one, found it giving way under him, and his feet being sucked down into apparently unfathomable abysses of watery moss. When he ceased sinking he was already considerably above his knees, and it soon became apparent that every effort to extricate himself only plunged him in deeper difficulties. So at last he ceased to struggle, and shouted lustily for help. Fortunately he had not long to wait for help, as it appeared soon in the shape of a "sweet Highland girl." She was not exactly Wordsworth's "Sweet Highland Girl," for it could hardly be said of her with truth that

> A very shower
> Of beauty is thine earthly dower.

And still less that she was

> A dancing shape, an image gay,
> To haunt, to startle, and waylay.

No. Maggie Macdonald, the shepherd's daughter, was a broad, substantial, solid, comely, good-natured Highland lassie, who, if she weighed a pound, weighed a good ten stone, and whose waist would have cut up into at least four waists of fashionable beauties. She had black hair, fine dark eyes, ruddy cheeks, and a wide, good-humoured mouth; and on the whole, though some fastidious critics might have objected that the degrees of latitude of her equatorial region were somewhat excessive, she was pleasant to the eye, and presented an attractive picture of good health, good nature, and good sense. That she possessed also a most solid *understanding* was apparent both when she kilted her petticoats up to the knee to wade through the mire to Fitzmuddle's rescue, and by the prompt and effectual measures which she took to effect that purpose.

Having waded to the firm bank of peat which was almost within reach of Fitzmuddle, "Tak' the cartridges out o' the gun," she said, "and gie me haud o' the end o' it."

This injunction being obeyed, the superiority of solid over showy qualities soon became apparent, for if Wordsworth's Highland girl, the fair vision of Inversnaid, had been at one end of the gun, and Fitzmuddle at the other, all the vision's shower of beauty would have been of little avail to extricate our hero from his perilous position.

But when it came to a real tug of war, Maggie's ten stone and solid understanding carried the day, and first one leg, then the other, came slowly out of the green bog with a pop like that of a gigantic soda-water bottle going off, and Fitzmuddle was half hauled and half scrambled to the bank of safety.

His gratitude to his fair benefactress was boundless, and was still further increased when she took him to a cottage by the side of the bog, and made the good wife, who was an acquaintance of hers, stir up the fire and put fresh peats on, and make him a cup of hot tea while his clothes were drying; after which charitable duties Maggie bade him good-bye and proceeded on her walk to her aunt's cottage near the foot of the glen, where she had some errands to do before returning to her father's in the evening.

But Fitzmuddle's debt of gratitude to this "sweet Highland girl" was not by any means exhausted, for once more before the day closed she saved him from a position of imminent peril.

After having rested and thoroughly dried himself, he looked out of the door of the cottage, and found that with a sudden change, the mist had cleared off, and the sun come out bright and hot ; so he started for the lodge, this time keeping on the firm ground, and intending to walk slowly across the moor on the chance of getting a shot at a curlew or a plover. Now whether the heat overcame him, or he felt tired after his wetting and struggles in the bog, I do not know, but when half-way across the moor, he sat down to rest in the shade of a huge boulder, almost the size of a small cottage, which had been dropped there by some retreating glacier or stranded iceberg in the far distant Glacial period. Here he smoked a contemplative cigar, gave one or two portentous yawns, and finally dropped off fast asleep.

How long he slept is uncertain, but he was awakened by a sound which to his confused senses seemed like the roaring of waves on a rock-bound shore, or the hoarse clamour of "bar one" from excited bookmakers. When he rubbed his eyes, however, and saw distinctly, a much more formidable apparition met them: that of a herd of wild Highland cattle, headed by a most unmistakably ferocious bull, who, drawn by curiosity, had closed in on him, and stood within twenty yards tossing their heads, waving their tails, pawing the ground, and giving vent to a series of angry bellowings.

If Fitzmuddle had been staking his whole fortune on a bear sale of Turks or Egyptians, he could not have felt more alarmed at the operations of the bulls. The leading bull especially, a shaggy black devil with wicked red eyes, was evidently bent on hoisting Fitzmuddle stock up to the highest possible premium.

What was to be done? He jumped on his feet, and his first movement was the signal for a general charge of the infuriated animals.

If there had been no Glacial period, what would have become of Fitzmuddle? Nay, what would have become of all of us?—for it is the ice plough which, in the temperate regions of the northern hemisphere, has done all the rough work of subsoil ploughing, which alone has rendered them habitable for agricultural, and therefore for civilised man. No less potent engine could have smashed up the solid rocks into loams and gravels, and spread a mantle of corn-producing soil over the bare bones of the earth.

But in this particular instance it was the boulder dropped on the solitary heath, which proved to Fitzmuddle a rock of ages and ark of salvation. For with a nimble alacrity inspired by the close proximity of tossing horns and bellowing mouths, he scrambled up it, and for the moment was in safety. For the moment only, for like Bazaine in Metz, he was closely beleaguered in his impregnable fortress, and no means of escape was left unless some friendly force should attack the enemy in the rear and raise the siege.

Such an ally appeared unexpectedly in the "sweet Highland girl," who, returning from her aunt's cottage after she had done her errands, passed that way and witnessed our hero's perilous predicament. Cattle were no terror to her, for she had often when a little lassie herded them, and driven them off the corn, and made herself a terror to them by stones skilfully hurled. And the feeling was reciprocal, for these half-wild creatures, who would have charged a red line of soldiers without hesitation, felt as much alarm at the sight of a girl with a stick in one hand and a stone in the other, as a mob of London roughs might do at the sudden apparition of a blue-coated policeman.   Accordingly, when Maggie shouted and threw a stone which hit the leading bull right between the eyes, the besieging army broke up and fled in as much consternation as did the army of the Grand Vizier, when Sobieski, the fiery king of battles, charged their lines before Vienna with his gallant handful of Polish lancers.

Thus twice in the same day did Fitzmuddle owe his deliverance from deadly danger to the "sweet Highland girl," the fair and substantial daughter of the shepherd's cottage, Maggie Macdonald.

CHAPTER V.

TROUT AND SALMON FISHING.

As the river continued too low for any chance of catching a salmon, Fitzmuddle determined to try his hand at the trout, and accompanied by the faithful Donald, walked one fine morning across the hill to the Loch of Foulis.

"Why do they call it Loch of Fools?" asked Fitzmuddle. "Is it because those who go there never catch anything, and are fools for their pains?"

"It's na fools," said Donald, "but Foulis; and I'm thinking it just got the name from the number of fouls, there's an awfu' lot of wild-fouls on it in winter, dukes and sic like fools."

Whatever may be the correct etymology, a

very beautiful loch was this of Foulis when you came on it as Fitzmuddle did, on a fine autumn morning. At the upper end great, rugged mountains rose in bare-ribbed rock from the dark, still waters; lower down, little promontories jutted out with rocks and boulders covered with fern and rich purple-blooming heather; and between them, little secluded bays, some of them with shores of bright shingle or yellow sand, on which the most brilliantly spotted and golden-coloured trout were wont to lie. Towards the lower end, where the river ran out, the lake was shallower, and a multitude of little islands, some mere stranded boulders, others large enough to support a growth of luxuriant heather and small birches and rowans, diversified its surface. The rocks were mostly of granite, and the crystals sparkled like diamonds in the sun; while here and there a grassy tongue of emerald green protruded itself into the lake.

When they first got to the creek where the boat was moored, it was quite calm, and the surface of the lake was dimpled over with the rings of rising trout ; but after waiting for half-an-hour, a cloud came over, dropping a slight shower, and sending a gentle breeze, so they hastily put up the rod, selected the flies, and pushed off from the shore.

It was a perfect day for fly-fishing, and novice as Fitzmuddle was, he succeeded in raising a trout at almost every cast, and now and then actually hooking and securing a small one. But his line splashed the water too much and frightened the big fish away, or if one did touch his fly under water, he was too slow in striking, and it got away. After losing two or three in this way, Donald said to him :

"Just shorten your line, sir, and let the wind tak' the flie and drop it gently down, and the moment you find the line check the least bit, strike sharp and ding it into him."

Following this advice, Fitzmuddle to his intense delight hooked two fish well on to one pound each, and after an exciting five minutes' play, Donald got them safely into the landing-net. But on the third attempt he came to sad grief, for throwing his line out just as they rounded the point of one of the little rocky islands, a sudden puff of wind blew it back into his face, and feeling the line check, he remembered Donald's advice and struck on the instant.

The result was that, in parliamentary phrase, "the Noes had it."

The nose had it. In this little phrase how many questions of deep moment are involved! Why does the first commoner of England, the Speaker of the House of Commons, invariably assume a habit of squinting when he mounts into the chair of dignity, in flowing robe and full-bottomed wig, as he certainly does, for he is constantly turning the Eyes (Ayes) to the right and the Nose (Noes) to the left? But this is a question of parliamentary procedure which, like many others, must always remain inscrutable. Why does that august assembly, potent to make and unmake Ministries, and sway the policy of an empire on which the sun

never sets, sit in hopeless imbecility or impotent
indignation, while some pretentious bore wastes
hour after hour with interminable talk, or inter-
poses motions for adjournment, or grievances
of some Irish whisky-seller or English vendor
of patent medicines, when the whole House
is impatient for a statement by a responsible
Minister affecting the honour of the nation, or
the security of its defences? Is the time of
Parliament, the most precious of its possessions,
the one thing over which it can exercise no
effective control, or is it the vested property of
some half-dozen gentlemen who wish to please
their constituents, and advertise their names
by seeing themselves in print next day in the
newspapers? Or why should the great mother
of Parliaments shrink from enforcing that decency
and decorum of manners which are observed
in every little mock parliament presided over
by a "Worthy Grand" or "Knight Commander
of the Order of Good Templars"?

These, however, are inscrutable mysteries;
let us turn rather to considerations in which it

is possible to discern some glimmering of light.
By pondering deeply we may perhaps discover
some analogy between the softly melting or
brightly gleaming eyes and the assent they
signify, and also between dissent and that supercilious feature which is curled up with disdain
and contradiction. No lover ever addressed his
mistress with

> Drink to me only with thy nose,
> And I will pledge with mine,

or failed to recognise his "ain lassie" by the
"kind blink that's in her ee."

Assuming, therefore, such a natural connection,
shall we ask what mighty issues in the world's
history have depended on these fundamental
features? Was it the Bourbon nose which caused
the French Revolution, and sent Charles Dix
to end his days at Holyrood? Had the nose
been less obstructively negative, and the eyes
prompter in assent, would the descendants of
Hugh Capet be still reigning over France, and
residing in the unburnt Tuileries? It has been
said that if Cleopatra's nose had been an inch

shorter the course of Roman history would have been different. Does this hold good also of the lengthy feature which gives expression to the refined and handsome, but vacillating and un-truthful face of Charles I. in the great equestrian portrait by Vandyke? With firmer lips, truer eyes, and a more aquiline or doggish frontal appendage, would the Stuart dynasty be now constitutional monarchs of a parliamentary England?

Again, what would be the condition of modern science and thought if those heavy-browed and doubtless heavy-nosed Inquisitors had succeeded in locking up Galileo's discoveries as well as his person in a dungeon of the Vatican?

It makes the brain reel to endeavour to trace the ever-widening circles of changes that may result in this strangely-complicated and strangely-connected universe, from causes apparently the most trivial. Not an act is done, not a word spoken, which, in the "boundless realm of un-ending change," may not turn out to be the touch of the finger which pulled the trigger, which exploded the dynamite, and shattered creeds, societies, and emperors into a thousand fragments.

To return, however, from these high-soaring speculations to the point from which we started—the hook in Fitzmuddle's nose—its extraction presented a problem of considerable difficulty. For when the barb has once become embedded in the flesh, it is no easy matter to pull it out the way it went in, as Launcelot experienced when Lavaine had to tug so. hard to draw out the lance which had pierced his side at the tournament. But that was a lance, and probably not barbed, so that Lavaine, by putting out all his strength, succeeded. Fitzmuddle's hook, how-ever, being barbed, it baffled all Donald's skill to extract it, and they had to send for the doctor, who forced the barb through the right way, nipped it off with a pair of pincers, and then drew the hook back without difficulty; so that beyond a slight swelling and disfigurement for a couple of days, Fitzmuddle was none the worse for the adventure.

At length the storm came, and for two days and nights it raged. The wind sweeping in furious gusts round the shoulder of Ben More, tore up the water of the gloomy loch into angry waves, and scattered it in showers of spray. Then came a lull, and the strong rain fell as if the heavens were one great shower-bath of which the demon of the gale had pulled the string. The windows of the lodge rattled, the roof leaked, and the stout Highland girl who acted as house-maid had hard work with mops and pails to arrest the little rivers that ran down the passages, and threatened to form a lake in the best sitting-room.

But all the mops and pails in the world would have been powerless to dry up the spongy peat-mosses and swollen tarns, which sent down so many raging burns into the roaring river, whose full torrent swept down in a wide stream of inky black water flecked with foam, over shallows where three days ago a child could have crossed.

At length on the third day the gale broke. The sullen pall of leaden-coloured clouds opened up, and patches of blue sky appeared, across which fragments of clouds, torn from the ragged-edged walls which still obscured the horizon, chased one another in rapid flight and disappeared to leeward. Their flight became slower, the patches of blue sky widened, and towards evening the sun came out in its glory just before sunset, lighting up the whole western sky with vivid tints of crimson and of gold.

The loch, a few hours ago dark as the mouth of hell, now glowed like the pavement of heaven, and the gray ghastly hills stood out in richest purple against the delicate tints of the evening sky. As night approached the mountain wall became more weird in its mysterious beauty, and the sky and sea, with a last flush of crimson glory, assumed the sober livery of night. With nightfall the wind quite died away, the stars came out twinkling in the transparent air, and rising suddenly into sight over the clear outline of the dark hills. The calm loch reflected the brighter constellations as in a mirror, and everything was as still and solemn as sleep or death, after the passionate excitement and turmoil of a day of struggle.

With early morn Donald was afoot to watch the river and report progress. At eight o'clock he opened Fitzmuddle's door, inserted his head and said : " Wauken up, sir, and get your breakfast. I'm thinking she'll fush the day."

Fitzmuddle, roused from the embraces of Morpheus, and still only half-awake, just caught the last words, and had an unpleasant suspicion that they referred to fresh proceedings on the part of a certain young lady, and that he, the Honourable Augustus, was the fish intended to be caught.

"Dear me," he said, "you don't say so! I thought the lady had enough of fishing to last her for her life the other day off the Butt of Mull."

Donald could not restrain a hearty laugh. "It's no o' the leddy I'm speaking, sir; it's o' the river. Get up and ye'll catch a bonny salmon."

"Oh, the river, is it?" said Fitzmuddle, greatly

relieved. "But tell me, Donald, why do you call the river 'she'?"

"It's just the way we have in the Hielands," said Donald, "it sounds mair kindly like; it gars you think o' a bonnie lassie, and that's aye a pleasant thought."

"Why, Donald," said Fitzmuddle, "I declare you are quite a poet; I should never have thought of such a thing, though now you say it, I do think it sounds nicer to call a river a 'she' than an 'it.'"

"Begging your honour's pardon," said Donald, "it's no your fault but your misfortune to be born a Saxon; if you had been born in the Hielands and had the Gaelic, that way of speaking would just have come natural to you."

However, further disquisition on the comparative merits of the Celtic and Saxon races was cut short by a plunge of Fitzmuddle, who, extricating himself from the bed-clothes, manfully rushed to the tub, and in due course descended to breakfast. Ham and eggs, a broiled chicken, and unlimited scones and marmalade, were the solid foundation on which he prepared himself for the labours of the day; and having tasted just the least nip of the mountain dew, and lighted a mild Havannah, he started with Donald for a five-mile tramp to the river, his heart glowing with ardour, in peace and goodwill with himself and all mankind, and humming as he walked to the old hunting melody, "This day a fish shall die." Indeed, it was a morning on which it was impossible to feel otherwise than happy, and Schopenhauer himself must have confessed that "pessimism," like most other "isms," had its exceptions and limitations.

The air, cleared by the storm, was so fresh and exhilarating that to inhale it was like breathing ethereal champagne. The gorse and heather glittered with dew-drops brighter than the brightest diamonds. The cocks and hens at every cottage door, who had stood huddled together so dismal and bedraggled during the two days' rain, were now scattered all over the place, preening their feathers, scratching for food, and crowing and cackling for sheer delight in the rays of the morning sun; while the ducks waddled along over every little plot of grass, hunting eagerly for the slugs and worms which were crawling about on the moistened surface. Higher up the hill an old cock grouse rose at their feet and flew away with a cheerful crow, and the wild cry of a couple of curlews was blended with the distant whistle of a flock of golden plovers.

Walking at a rapid pace, for Fitzmuddle's long legs and slender frame enabled him almost to keep up with the stronger Donald, they soon topped the ridge, and breaking into a run down the opposite slope, they soon reached the river. It had gone down a good deal since yesterday, though still brimming up to the banks, and presenting a formidable succession of deep pools and foaming rapids. The inky blackness of the water had toned down into a clear amber, or rather the colour of a celestial and spiritualised Guinness's Stout; in which, as Donald observed, "No weel-conditioned salmon could help rising at the first flie that cam' ower him."

Fitzmuddle watched with eager interest the operations of putting up the rod and fastening on the casting-line, and bent all the attention of his mighty mind to the sage remarks of Donald touching the selection of a proper fly.

"I'm thinking," said Donald, "that this Joc Scott is about the right thing. The water's big, and she'll stand a good-sized flie and a bright ane, though the day be fine."

Accoutred for the fray, Fitzmuddle grasped the rod and stepped down briskly to the bank of the river Donald had selected as a likely spot to begin with: a wide pool, flowing deep on the far side under a curving bank of rock, while on the near side a shelving bank of gravel, dry in fine weather, sloped gently downwards. A rapid stream poured through a chasm of rocks at the upper end, which gradually died away into rippling eddies towards the tail of the pool, and finally ran out in a smooth but rapid stream, until it fell in a cascade of some twenty feet in height, through another rocky chasm into the next pool. Fitzmuddle wielded his rod and

manfully essayed to cast his' fly into the stream.
But easy as casting a salmon fly seems to be on
paper, it is not quite so easy in practice. The
slow, steady sweep of the practised angler is not
at once attained by a nervous beginner, and the
cracking off of sundry flies, and knotting the
line into inextricable tangles, are experiences
which have to be gone through before the first
elements of the art are fairly mastered. However,
Donald was at his elbow with sage advice.

"Just remember 'make ready,' 'present,'
'fire,'" he said. "'Make ready,' when your cast is
finished and you are going to lift your flie;
'present,' when ye throw it fairly back behint ye;
then pause a second, and when you say 'fire,' bring
the rod forward with a smart but steady cast."

Fitzmuddle possessed the first attribute for
a ready learner of this as well as of more
important matters, the noble humility which is
conscious of its own imperfections and not
ashamed to learn. Whether in casting a fly or
in the more arduous experiences of practical
life, the surest road to failure is to be too

conceited to know that you have failed, and too impatient to recognise that docility and perseverance are safer guides than any amount of fancied heaven-born genius.

Accordingly, after a few unsuccessful attempts, Fitzmuddle managed to flop out some yards of line into the stream, and although the fly fell with a considerable splash, a salmon in the taking humour is not so easily alarmed as the shy speckled trout of a clear chalk stream, and has no idea of being balked of his purpose by such a trifle as a clumsy cast. At his third cast the fly floated down the stream until the line became straight, and Fitzmuddle was in the act of lifting it for another cast, when he was conscious of an obstruction. At first he thought his fly had caught a rock, and he jerked it sharply to release it. Luckily the tackle was sound, and the jerk only served to fix the hook firmly in the jaws of a fine salmon, whose silver side as he gave a plunge on feeling the steel, sent a throb of excitement tingling through every vein of the astonished angler.

"Gie him line, for gudeness' sake gie him line, and haud up the point of your rod," shouted the equally excited Donald, as the salmon darted with one rush from the bottom to the top of the pool. "Reel him in, reel, reel for your life," again shouted Donald, as the fish turned and ran down stream for the deeper water, where for a time he sulked and remained stationary.

A stone thrown in by Donald started him off, and he began dashing about the pool wildly, and twice sprang high out of the water, showing the goodly proportions of a clean-run fish of at least fifteen or sixteen pounds.

"Eh, mon, he's a grand fush," said Donald, "be canny wi' him; keep your rod up, and reel up a' you can, and he'll soon be spent."

And no doubt an experienced angler would soon have had him within reach of the gaff, but Fitzmuddle was inexperienced and excited, and in spite of Donald's admonitions gave the fish far too much of his own way, and half the time the line was quite slack, giving the salmon time to get second wind and renew the fight. At length,

after about twenty minutes of this work, Fitzmuddle's arms, unused to this strain on their
muscles, became quite stiff, and to relieve them he
lowered his right hand and brought his left close
to his breast. Horror of horrors! the line caught
in a bunch of keys, lockets, and other useless nick-
nacks, which it was one of Fitzmuddle's youthful
weaknesses to wear with his watch-chain. It
snapped, the bent rod flew up, and the salmon
disappeared with a final leap and a flourish of his
tail which Fitzmuddle felt as a personal insult, and
was wont in future years to aver that the salmon,
heaping insult upon injury, distinctly winked at
him with its left eye as it plunged into the pool.

There are many disappointments in life. It is
unpleasant to have your favourite article returned
to you by an editor, and your pet picture rejected
by the hanging committee; and worse still for a
fashionable young lady in her sixth London season,
who has just brought a rich baronet to the verge
where she thinks his next sentence must be a proposal, to see him take up his hat and wish her
good morning with a commonplace compliment.

Nor is the position of an ardent youth altogether to be envied, who having screwed his courage up to the point of popping the question, sees his fair *innamorata*, like Mistress Jean in the ballad of the laird of Cockpen :

> Say, Na,
> And drop a low curtsy and turn awa'.

But believe me, reader, these pangs, though more enduring, are less sharp for the moment than the sensation of the angler who, one moment fast in a fine salmon, in the next finds that he is gone, and not without an inward suspicion that some bungling of his own may be responsible for the fiasco.

Fitzmuddle was simply frantic. He stamped and danced about on the gravel, and at length threw himself down at full length, and declared that he would renounce fishing for ever and a day.

"Donald," said he, "do you know what one of the wisest men in the world said of fishing ?— that it was just a stick and a string, with a fish at one end and a fool at the other."

"Aweel, sir," replied Donald, "ye maunna be downhearted; that saying can't apply to you, for whatever may be the case at the one end, I am sure there is nae fish at the tother."

Comforted by this assurance, Fitzmuddle lighted a cigar to compose his ruffled nerves, and finally agreed to follow Donald's advice and go to a smaller pool, a couple of hundred yards higher up, where there was a good chance of a grilse, leaving the big pool to rest for half-an-hour before trying it again for another large fish.

His perseverance was rewarded, for in the upper pool he really did succeed in catching a handsome grilse weighing six pounds. It was not a very artistic performance, but the tackle was strong, the fish well hooked, and Fitzmuddle hauled him by main strength, after the first rush, within reach of Donald's gaff.

Inspired by this success, Fitzmuddle, full of the hope that "springs eternal in the human breast," returned to the deep pool and stood eager for the fray.

"Just try if you canna cast a yard or two

further," said Donald; "the big fish are very apt
to lie just on the far side of the stream.   But
whatever you do, be careful in wading, for the
gravel bank goes down varra steep after you are
about ten yards out."

Fitzmuddle waded out with due caution, and
made repeated though ineffectual attempts to cast
his fly well beyond the stream.   At length a fine
salmon made a splendid rise, rolling over his broad
back, which to Fitzmuddle's delighted eyes looked
as big as that of a porpoise, just about a yard
beyond the spot he had reached with his longest
cast.   Fired by the sight, he forgot Donald's warning, and tried to gain the extra yard by venturing
to wade a little deeper.

Alas! alas! "facilis descensus Averni," easy
is the downward slope that leads to destruction;
"sed revocare gradus," but to redeem lost character
and missed opportunities, or, as in Fitzmuddle's
case, to regain a firm footing on a steep slope
of sand which is slipping away from under your
feet, "hic labor hoc opus est," this is a different
affair altogether, a work to be accomplished, only

by painful effort, and often not at all without the aid of a friendly redeemer. So Fitzmuddle found it, for getting deeper and deeper as the sand slipped away, he made one tremendous effort to regain firm footing, which, like the last throw of many a desperate gambler, only consummated his ruin, for the treacherous sand gave way altogether, and in the twinkling of an eye he found himself immersed in the rushing water.

Now let me tell those who have never experienced such a catastrophe, that there are few positions more full of danger than to find yourself carried down by a rapid river with wading trousers on. Unless you are a good swimmer, and preserve perfect presence of mind, you have an excellent chance of being drowned. If you attempt to swim on your breast, up go your legs buoyed by the air in your waterproof trousers, and down consequently goes your head. Your only salvation is to turn on your back, bend it well, and strike downwards with your hands so as to keep your head above water, and kick out with your legs so as to get near enough to the shore to regain your footing, or catch hold of something on the bank. I once knew a man who, in such a predicament, took things so coolly, that he not only brought himself safely to land, but kept hold of his rod, and never even extinguished the lighted cigar he had in his mouth. But Fitzmuddle had neither the practice nor the presence of mind necessary for such a performance, and with the first plunge he got his head under, his mouth full of water, and floated, splashing and struggling, down the stream that was hurrying towards its leap over the rocky fall. Once over the brink of that fall, his only chance of escape from drowning lay in the contingency that his brains might be dashed out against the boulders before the water had quite completed its work.

However, let me hasten to reassure the nerves of my readers, and especially of my fair readers. My novel is not a chamber of horrors, and ends happily. Fitzmuddle was saved, as it were, from the very jaws of death, and underwent many more adventures both of flood and field. It happened in the following manner:

The wonderful relation between Spirit and Matter has long been a problem for the greatest intellects. How certain molecular vibrations translate themselves into transport, others into agony, how soul, conscience, and all the diviner attributes of human nature are inseparably connected with mechanical combinations of oxygen, hydrogen, and other atoms, is indeed an insoluble mystery. Nevertheless, learned philosophers have arrived at this result, that certain faculties and emotions are apparently located in certain separate regions of the bodily frame. Thus the brain is said to be the seat of intelligence, the heart of love, and another portion of the human form divine, which it is unnecessary to describe more minutely, is, by common consent, considered to be the seat of honour. Why it should be so is not very apparent, unless it be on the principle of giving the broadest possible basis to that which is the primary and most solid foundation of all real excellence of character, self-reverence, or a keen sense of personal honour.

Be this as it may, Fitzmuddle on this critical

occasion realised to the fullest extent the truth of the poet's saying, that "the seat of honour is the seat of safety," for as he floated down the stream, face downwards, this portion of his person, projecting above the turbid torrent, presented what Archimedes so much desired, a fulcrum or point of attachment against which force might be profitably exerted. With singular presence of mind Donald had grasped the situation at a glance. On the very verge of the fall, where the roaring torrent plunged twenty feet down over rugged boulders into the dark and gloomy pool below, a ledge of rock just afforded foothold for a single foot, while a dwarfed and misshapen birch overhung the stream, and twined its gnarled roots firmly among the crevices of the rocky bank. Grasping this with his left hand, and holding the gaff firmly in his right, Donald stretched out as far as he could over the water and waited for the approach of the floating form of his unfortunate master. It was no time to stand on ceremony. In another second, Fitzmuddle would have been over the fall, and his sporting adventures would

have come to a sad termination. Accordingly
Donald struck his gaff in with a right good will,
and, as the javelin of Diomed pierced through
the shield of triple bull-hide and brazen cuirass
of the God of War, so did the sharp point of
the gaff penetrate through the wading trousers
and under garments, until it bit deeply into the
tender flesh, which luckily proved tough enough
to enable Donald to tow the half-drowned Fitzmuddle to the shore and lift him up the bank,
thus realising what most salmon anglers have
experienced, that a "clever gaffer often saves a
good fish."

With equal promptitude Donald propped his
master up against a sloping bank, got out the
whisky flask, poured half of its contents down
Fitzmuddle's throat, and soaking a handful of
soft moss in the other half, applied it to the
wound inflicted by the gaff, and bound it tightly
up with his handkerchief. The effect of this
double application of whisky, tingling in the
inside and smarting on the outer cuticle, soon
restored Fitzmuddle to his senses, and to the

honest Donald's delight he opened his eyes and began to inquire where he was and what had happened to him.

When this was explained to him he was fervent in his thanks to his rescuer, and vowed that whatever favour Donald might ever have occasion to ask of him, should be freely granted. The problem then came up for serious discussion how he was to get back to the lodge, for any attempt to walk, or even to rise, brought on fresh bleeding from the wound to such an extent, that although Fitzmuddle pluckily attempted it, it was manifestly unsafe to persevere. Donald, however, proved equal to the occasion, for wrapping Fitzmuddle in his plaid, he took him up in his strong arms as if he had been a baby, and carried him to the nearest cottage, where a cart was procured in which the wounded hero was deposited on a bed of rough hay and safely conveyed to the lodge.

For several days he was confined to the sofa, but youth, a good constitution, and diachylon plaster work wonders, and he was soon restored to his wonted health and spirits. Physical wounds are far more easily cured than those deeper wounds which are inflicted, so often carelessly, by "evil tongues, rash judgments, and the sneers of selfish men;" and the diachylon plaster has yet to be invented which will heal the scars of a sensitive soul, stabbed by cruel words and ungenerous actions.

CHAPTER VI.

DEER-STALKING—THE SHEPHERD'S COTTAGE.

ONE morning at six o'clock in the first week of October, Donald put his head inside the door of Fitzmuddle's bedroom in a state of great excitement, and said: "The shepherd has sent word that a fine stag was seen last night in the gloaming, a good way on our side of the march, and he really thinks it was the muckle stag o' Ben More ; so get up, if you please, sir, and we'll be off and after him."

Fitzmuddle jumped out of bed, made a hasty breakfast, and mounting two of the shooting ponies, he and Donald started for the shepherd's cottage to get more precise information. The morning was dull and lowering and the mist hung low on the hills, but inspired by the prospect of a stalk they did not mind the weather.

On arriving at the cottage Sandy Macdonald, the old shepherd, told them that the stag had certainly come down from the mountain to the Muir of Myrie, a great flat expanse of peat moss, stunted heather, and coarse rusty-coloured grass, which stretched for some miles along the foot of the Ben More range, and he described the locality, about four miles off, where he had last seen him.

" Eh, mon," he said, "he was a grand beast, he looked as big as a horse last night through the mist, and I never saw sic a head; he must have twelve or fourteen tines at the varra least."

They pushed forward, full of hope of bringing this grand head back to the cottage before night, and counting the tines at their leisure; but deer-stalking is not all pleasure, for when they got fairly on to the Muir of Myrie, the wet, clammy mist came down so low that they could not see thirty yards ahead.

" It will never do to gae on in this mist," said Donald, " we should be sure to gie the beast our wind, and he'd be off across the march before we saw him."

"What's to be done, then?" said Fitzmuddle. "Surely you don't mean to give him up?"

"Na, na," said Donald, "but we must just sit down and wait till it clears up a bit. Maybe it will come on to rain in the afternoon, and then we may be able to see something."

So they sat down under the lee of a peat-hag, and passed the weary hours as they best could, until about two o'clock, when, as Donald predicted, the mist turned to good heavy rain, and though it still hung low on the mountain-side, it cleared a good deal off the flat muir. Donald took a good spy, but could see nothing.

"We must gae on another mile or twa," he said, "for it's likely the stag will ha' moved a bit across the muir since last night."

So they struggled and splashed on over the sloppy ground for twenty minutes or so, when they lay down behind a little hillock, and Donald took another long spy. Carefully he swept the horizon round with his glass, but at last he stopped.

"Do you see anything?" asked the excited Fitzmuddle.

"I'm no quite sure," said Donald, "but I thocht I saw something varra like him at the far side o' the muir. I'll just wipe the glass and tak' another look."

He did so, and after a long, steady look, said in a low voice :

"Sure enough it's him, I can make him out quite plainly now, and a grand beast he is."

"Where, where?" said Fitzmuddle; "let me look."

But it is one of the lessons that a novice in deer-stalking has to learn, that an inexperienced eye may look through a glass for a week and see nothing, where the practised eye of his stalker can almost count the points on the stag's head. So Fitzmuddle could only see something which might be either a tuft of withered fern, a boulder, or a stag, for any difference he could discern.

"He'll no be easy to get at," said Donald, "he's out on the flat muir, and the wind blowing right to him, so we'll have to gang a long way round, and be very canny in creeping, to win anywhere near him."

So he took the bearings of the spot very carefully, and crept back for about two hundred yards
from the hillock, till they got into one of those
channels in the moss which are worn by the
incessant rains, under shelter of which they commenced their stalk in a wide circle of fully two
miles, so as to get round to leeward of the stag,
and then crawl up, head to wind, as nearly as
possible to the place where they had marked
him.

Running with bent back across sloppy ground
in a heavy shower of rain, and every now and then
flopping into pools of black peat water, or sinking
up to the knees in treacherous morasses, is a mode
of taking one's pleasure sadly, which I suppose
few French sportsmen would appreciate who go
out in the glory of a chasseur's costume, with
fringed game-bag and feather in Tyrolese hat,
to pot at thrushes and blackbirds. But this
was nothing to what they had to endure when,
having completed their circuit, they had to crawl
the last quarter of a mile up wind. For now
instead of walking or running with bent back,

they had to assume the mode of progression
of the old serpent who so fortunately deceived
Eve, and delivered her descendants from that
garden of Eden, where, I think, they would have
been horribly bored, and to crawl and wriggle on
their stomachs, along slushy runlets, and over
spongy moss, and through streaming grass and
heather. At last Donald called a halt, for, as
ill-luck would have it, the mist came down again
thicker than ever.

"I daurna gang a yard further," he said,
"we're close on to the spot where I marked him;
we must just wait where we are, and perhaps
about sunset the mist will lift again."

To Donald this was a matter of indifference,
for he was like a water-dog, and accustomed to
be wet rather oftener than he was dry; but Fitzmuddle felt very miserable. As long as he was
in motion he was all right, and the excitement
kept him up; but when it came to be a question
of lying for an hour or two, half in water and
half in wet peat, with his teeth chattering in his
head and his bones chilled to the marrow, it is

no wonder that he found himself asking whether "le jeu vaut la chandelle." Even the solace of a cigar was denied him, for Donald whispered there was no knowing how near they might be to the beast, and a whiff of the scent of tobacco might start him off. So a nip of whisky was all the comfort he could get, and for a long while it looked very much as if all their pains would be undertaken for nothing, for the mist kept thick and night was fast approaching.

But just as the sun set, a sickly gleam appeared in the west, and the mist lifted. Donald peered cautiously over the bank of the peat-hag in which they were lying, and drew his head back carefully.

"He's within fifty yards," he said; "ye canna miss him."

Fitzmuddle peeped through a bunch of heather, and there stood the noble animal quite close. He had been lying down during the rain, and when that gleam had come at sunset, he had risen and turned his head towards it, and stood stretching himself out, and yawning, if stags ever do yawn, with his broadside fairly exposed at a distance of certainly not over sixty yards.

Donald shoved the cocked rifle cautiously forward into Fitzmuddle's hands and whispered:

"Take steady aim, and draw a fine bead just behind the shoulder, right for his heart."

Fitzmuddle did his best to follow these instructions; but whether his hand shook from the cold, or from the excitement with which his heart was bumping against his breast, or whether the rifle carried a trifle high at short ranges, will never be known, the only certainty about the matter being that when the smoke cleared off which hung low and heavy in the damp air, all that could be discerned was the tail and hind quarters of a magnificent stag in the act of disappearing over an adjoining brae.

"Clean missed him, by God!" exclaimed Donald. "Dash it; what a pity!" But in the next moment, with true Highland politeness, he thought of Fitzmuddle's wounded feelings, and added: "But it's nae altogether your fault, sir, for I'm thinking that was just the muckle stag o' Ben More himself, and the folks a' say he's no canny, and the bullet must be cast o' siller that's to bring him down."

Whether Fitzmuddle believed this or not, or whether he felt so utterly wretched as to be indifferent to the buffets of fate, I do not know; but I know this, that he took the escape of the stag much more philosophically than he did the loss of that first salmon who so wickedly winked at him.

Even in after life, though he did not always miss his stags, he never took so cordially to stalking as he did to other branches of sport, and soon gave it up altogether. You may think it soft of him, but although the stalk was exciting, and the moment of pulling the trigger one of intense interest, he did not like seeing, what so often happens, the poor beast going on with its entrails hanging out, or hobbling on three legs, and finally, when it was brought to bay by the dog and shot down, lying on the heather, with the limbs, a few minutes ago so springy and full of life, giving their last convulsive kicks, and the great human-looking eye turned reproachfully on you, and slowly glazing over with the films of death. And then there is that horrid butchering business of gralloching, which a man must be a born Highlander to stand.

It is a curious instance of the inconsistency of the human mind that a man should feel sentimental over the sorrows of a stag, who slaughters any number of grouse or pheasants without scruple or remorse. He never thinks of the wounded birds who get away, and doubtless have a very "mauvais quart d'heure," until some beneficent hawk or friendly fox puts a short end to their agony. I suppose, after all, humanity resolves itself into selfishness, and we pity only those creatures who come near enough to ourselves to enable the imagination to see some reflection of human suffering in their expiring struggles. The stag is such a mass of vigorous vitality that its death affects us almost as if we saw the athletic Highlander, whose elastic step on the heather guided us in the stalk, struck suddenly dead. And the full eye has an expression which suggests human feelings of pain, terror, and upbraiding; while the grouse is too remote from us to excite similar feelings, and as for the salmon, with the exception of that wink which Fitzmuddle vouched for with more and more positiveness every year as time rolled on, we never heard of its eye conveying any suggestion of human emotion.

However, Fitzmuddle and Donald, trudging through the wet for six weary miles, thought much more of reaching the friendly shelter of the shepherd's cottage than of any such refined speculations, and right glad they were when at last they saw its lights gleaming through the darkness. Once within the door, their troubles were ended, for Maggie, foreseeing the plight in which they would arrive, had piled on the peats and made a blazing fire both but and ben, and laid out the shepherd's suit of Sunday clothes as a change for Fitzmuddle, and got a pot ready with three fowls and some slices of ham, and potatoes, and onions, and cabbage, all ready to put on the fire when they came in, and in the meantime the kettle boiling to give them a cup of tea, or glass of hot toddy, as they might prefer, while supper was getting ready.

The shepherd's clothes were safe to fit Fitzmuddle on the principle upon which the hat and wig of his friend the Calendar fitted John Gilpin, viz. :

> " My head is twice as big as yours,
> Therefore they needs must fit,"

for, indeed, the shepherd was about two inches taller and two feet more in circumference than Fitzmuddle. So he got into dry clothes, had a cup of hot tea, and sat down in an arm-chair before the fire enjoying the appetising smell that came from the mess boiling in the adjoining kitchen, in a state of supreme comfort. As for Donald, after much blushing and giggling on the part of Maggie, and protestations on his part that wet clothes never hurt a Hielandman, he was persuaded to put on a pair of dry trousers and stockings, and take off his wet coat and wrap a blanket about his shoulders.

Fitzmuddle often looked back on this day's adventures with pleasure, for we are so constituted that the recollections on which we like to dwell in after days, are not those of ease and comfort, but of hardship and privation. I often fancy myself in the Bay of Biscay, hove to in a heavy south-west gale on board one of the P. and O. steamers, and see the great mountainous waves of deep indigo blue, flecked with foam, rolling in, and sometimes, when a ray of sickly sunlight struggled through the drifting clouds, green-glimmering towards the summit before they curled over in a cascade of brilliant white. On that voyage we were said to have broken £100 worth of crockery, and the spectacle of the stewards staggering in with the dishes at dinner was that of good men struggling with difficulties; while every mouthful had to be snatched at the turn of one of those rolls which converted horizontal into perpendicular. Yet the remembrance of those three days is a green spot in my memory, while the many good dinners I have eaten, and the soft beds I have slept in, have all faded away.

So also in matters less material than rolling waves or misty mountains, we like best to recall

those passages of our lives in which we stood face
to face with dangers and difficulties, and looked
straight into their eyes, and either by supply
avoiding or grimly encountering them, vanquished
them and threw them fairly behind us. Life is
made up of contrasts, and is fullest for those who,
like Ulysses, have ever

> Enjoyed greatly and suffered greatly,

and more lives are rusted to death by disuse
than are broken in the keen sword-play of polished
blades.

Fitzmuddle's reflections, however, did not get
beyond the sensation of intense animal enjoyment
as he stretched his legs before the fire after making
a hearty supper on Maggie's miscellaneous stew,
which he ever afterwards pronounced to be the
ne plus ultra of the art of cookery. The shepherd
and Donald wanted to leave him in the best room
in solitary dignity, but he would not hear of it,
and insisted on their coming in and having a glass
of whisky toddy, and a smoke and comfortable
crack altogether, before they went to bed.

They did so, and the talk happened to turn on the Crofter question, which was then exciting much attention. Old Macdonald, the shepherd, was great on the subject of their grievances.

"Where would the lairds have been," he said, "if the men of the clan had not won the land by the sword and held it? It's no for me to speak against sheep, who makes my living by them, but it is gae hard to see men turned off the land like nowt, just because woo' gaes up, or some rich gentleman from the South bids a high rent to mak' a deer forest."

But Donald was all for emigration.

"What you say is true enough, Sandy," he said; "but there's many a hard thing in this world. It was hard on the auld Picts when the Gael turned them out o' their land; and on the Macdougalls when they lost their holdings to Macdonalds and Campbells just because their chief took the wrang side in Bruce's wars. But it's nae good whining over things; we must just take them as we find them and make the best of them. 'Set a stiff heart to a stey brae,' ye ken, and dinna stop at hame starving and grumbling on wee patches o' stanes and moss, that are na fit to keep a decent cow on, when there's plenty o' good land and good wages to be got in America."

"Yes," said Fitzmuddle, "and what says the Scripture : 'Increase and multiply and replenish the earth.' You would not go against Scripture, Sandy, and say that a whole continent is to be left to buffaloes and red Indians, instead of supporting millions of hardy, industrious, God-fearing men and women, just because Highlanders and Irishmen cling to their native hills and bogs like children to their nurses' aprons?"

"Weel, weel, sir," said Sandy, "I canna deny it, and it's na for me to gang against Scripture; but it's hard on a man for a' that to leave the glen where he was brought up, and go among strange places and strange faces."

"Why," said Fitzmuddle, "all the races that have ever been worth anything in history have been great emigrants. Look at the old Norsemen and the modern Scotchmen. What are you

K 2

Highlanders but the descendants of a set of Irish who emigrated long ago? You know that Ireland was called Scotia and the Irishmen Scoti in the time of the Romans."

This was a staggering argument, to which Sandy made no reply, so Fitzmuddle pushed his advantage and said:

"Now tell me truly, Sandy, if you had your life to live over again, would it not have been better for you to go while you were young, to a country where you might by this time have owned a fine farm of your own, instead of herding sheep for another on the mountain side?"

"Maybe it might," said Sandy, "but then you see I married when I was quite young, and though the Lord in His mercy took the wife now six years past, I had a sair lot of bairns, and a man wi' a lot o' bairns canna just be off as if he were a single lad like Donald here."

"But why did you marry so young?" said Fitzmuddle. "If you had waited a bit you might not have had such a sair lot of bairns, and might have saved money enough to take the wife and all of them to America."

"Weel, you see, sir," said Sandy, "I was bred as a shepherd, and it's gae lonely up in the hills, and there's just twa things we shepherds maun fain hae."

"What are they?" asked Fitzmuddle.

"Wives and tobacco," said Macdonald; and then putting his head a little on one side, he added contemplatively, "But maistly tobacco."

They all laughed, and having finished his toddy and being pretty well tired, Fitzmuddle turned into the box bed, which was a sort of dark hole in the wall, and in a minute was fast asleep. So also did the shepherd; but Donald and Maggie had apparently some interesting communications to make to one another, or why did they sit so long over the fire and discourse in whispers, and why were their heads in such close proximity, and when at last they said good night, and rose to part, why was Maggie's face so red? I suppose it was the fire. But was it the fire that made Donald, when he stepped out, look up at the stars and heave a sigh before he turned in among the dry heather beside the ponies, or was it that the Highland nature is full of a sort of instinctive poetry unknown to the more solid or stolid Saxon?

Fitzmuddle slept the sleep of the righteous till the first rays of the morning began to stream in through the narrow slit which did duty for a window, and then he woke with a curious tingling sensation all over him.

"Good Lord!" he said, "is it possible that I have got the Scotch itch? They say it comes of eating oatmeal, and I have been eating a deal of porridge lately."

Then he looked out, and on the floor he saw the shepherd's two collie dogs; one was scratching his ear with his hind leg as if for dear life, the other had his head turned round and his nose inserted in the fur of his back and wrinkled up in the energetic pursuit of some unseen enemy.

"Surely it can't be the Scotch itch," said Fitzmuddle, "the two dogs can't have caught it in the night."

Then he rubbed his eyes and saw, horror of horrors! a great spider suspended by a single thread from the ceiling within an inch of his nose, and legions of little crawling things on the blanket, which to his excited fancy seemed as big as black-beetles or small shrimps, and to be advancing steadily towards him in two well-formed columns of attack.

He jumped out of bed and rushed out into the clear morning air. The sun had not quite risen, but

> The sanguine sunrise with its meteor eyes
> And burning plumes outspread,

was just lighting up the edges of the light clouds floating near the horizon with crimson and with gold. The air, after yesterday's rain, was deliciously fresh, and clear, and pure, and the purple hills stood out in strong contrast against the delicate ethereal blue of the eastern sky. The mountains themselves and the moor lay in shade, dark, fresh, and dewy, like a new-made world, as you see them in Guido's fresco of Aurora. A little burn rippled down behind the cottage, and fell in a tiny cascade over a ledge of granite rock, making a deep, clear pool below, in which Fitz-muddle took a dip. The fresh cold water greatly allayed the cuticular irritation, and he came in with an excellent appetite for breakfast, and, forgetting his alarm about the Scotch itch, began by laying a solid foundation in the shape of a bowl of oatmeal porridge with a jug of delicious cream.

Breakfast over, he and Donald rose to depart, and mindful of the shepherd's aphorism of the previous evening respecting the superior solace of tobacco, he asked him to accept a sovereign to buy himself a good stock for the winter of his favourite luxury.

Macdonald at first declined, and protested it was far too much, and that he did not wish to be paid anything for a night's lodging. But on being pressed he reflected that it would not be altogether polite to refuse a gentleman's offer, and that there was a good deal of smoking in a sovereign's worth of tobacco, so he ended by accepting it.

"Many thanks, sir," he said, "and I hope you have been comfortable a' the night."

"Very much so," said Fitzmuddle, "only you introduced me to rather a scratch lot of acquaintance, whose too familiar attentions were not altogether acceptable."

"Me introduce you to acquaintance?" said Macdonald, with open-mouthed surprise. "I dinna ken what you mean."

"Why," said Fitzmuddle, "they were such a scratch lot that you see I have not done scratching myself yet."

Sandy gave a great laugh and said: "Oh, it's the fleas your honour means; we dinna make much account o' fleas in these parts, there's aye plenty o' them."

So they shook hands and parted excellent friends, but before he left, Fitzmuddle made another present, that of a handsome cairngorm broach to Maggie, which he had sent for to Oban, with instructions that it was to be the biggest and finest the jeweller had, on purpose to present to her as a token of gratitude for her double rescue of him from the bog and from the bulls. Maggie blushed and curtseyed her thanks, and Fitzmuddle held her by the hand rather longer than was strictly necessary, and when he bid her good-bye, told her she must be sure to come down to her aunt's and dance with him at the gillies' ball, which he intended to give before taking his departure from Mull.

Now by this broach there hangs a tale, but we must defer telling it till the next chapter.

CHAPTER VII.

THE GILLIES' BALL.

MAGGIE would not have been a true daughter of Eve if, next day being Sunday, she had not worn that splendid broach when she went to the Free Kirk; nor would Flora Fraser have been one if she had not observed it.

Flora was a tall, strapping, and not bad-looking Highland lass, daughter of the little shop-keeper in the Clachan, with whom Donald may have had some slight passing flirtation before he lost his heart to Maggie.

It was scarcely in human nature, therefore, that Flora should entertain any very friendly feelings towards Maggie, and seeing the broach, she at once had a shrewd suspicion where it came from, for some rumours of Fitzmuddle's adventures in the bog and with the bullocks had reached the Clachan, and as usual in such cases, not without considerable exaggerations, so that winks and nudges had already passed among its female population, and tongues had already begun to wag, and wonder what the English gentleman could see in a great hulk of a shepherd's lass like Maggie Macdonald.

Donald had not been to kirk that Sunday, for though he would like to have met Maggie, to tell the truth he was so keen about that muckle stag, that he neglected both his devotional duties and the attractions of his sweetheart, and spent that Sunday on the march seeing if he could spy anything of that mighty monarch of the glen. So when Flora met him next day, he was altogether ignorant of the broach and everything appertaining thereto.

Flora accosted him : " Weel, Donald, I suppose you have been saving up a' your siller to buy that grand broach for Maggie she cam' to the kirk wi'."

"What broach?" said Donald, "I ken nae-thing aboot it."

"Oh," said Flora, "if you did na gie it to her we ken wha did. It's no every lass that gets presents o' broaches from fine English gentlemen; tho' if you dinna mind it's nae business o' ours, tho' a' the Clachan are talking o' the way she is carrying on with Mr. Fitzmuddle."

It is wonderful what a deal of mischief that little implement the tongue can do, when it is set a-wagging to spread a tale of scandal. To be sure, if young men and young women would only be reasonable, and have a frank and friendly word of explanation with one another, they might pretty well defy

Evil tongues, rash judgments, and the sneers of selfish men;

but then young men and young women will not be reasonable, and especially when they are in love. Love seems to tighten up all the chords of emotion in the heart to such a high pitch that the slightest touch will often make one of them snap, and instead of giving forth sweet melody, pop! it goes off with a loud, discordant crack.

So in this case, if Donald had only had the sense to wait till he saw Maggie, and then ask her in a friendly way to tell him all about Fitzmuddle and the broach, she would have told him, what was the honest truth, that she loved his little finger better than all the bodies of all the fine gentlemen in England, and they would have kissed and been friends, and had a hearty laugh at Flora and her little malicious tittle-tattlings. But Donald, like a foolish fellow, felt jealous, and like Othello, found

> In trifles light as air,
> Confirmation strong as holy writ.

And when he next met Maggie he took what was about the worst course possible with a high-spirited girl, that of innuendo and hinting suspicion.

"I suppose you winna condescend to dance wi' a plain laddie at this gillies' ball," said he, "noo that you ha' gotten sic a braw broach frae a fine gentleman?"

Maggie fired up, as was natural, and replied:

"I will just dance wi' any one I like, and if

you choose to be jealous about nothing, you can dance a' the night wi' Flora Fraser."

So when the night of the ball came, though all the rest were uproariously happy, there was one there who was glum and miserable, and Maggie, though she seemed in high spirits, and did her best to initiate Fitzmuddle into the mysteries of the Highland fling, kept casting occasional glances towards Donald; and when, after drinking an extra tumbler or two of whisky toddy, he did, just out of bravado, stand up for a reel with Flora Fraser, you may be sure that made things no better but rather worse.

But the others had no such cares to oppress them, and the fun waxed fast and furious. The village piper came out in all the glory of full Highland dress, with his bagpipes all streaming with ribbons, and blew away till his face got as red as a turkey-cock—or as we call it in Scotland, a bubbly-jock—and his cheeks swelled out until you thought they must burst. And the fiddler, whom Fitzmuddle had got over from Tobermory, scraped with such vigour that his elbow ached again.

The lads and lasses, aye, and the middle-aged men and buxom dames, whooped and shouted and stamped on the floor, and tossed their legs and arms high in air, like that Miller Rab who, in the old song, was

Fidgen fain,
To dance the Highland fling.

And when the "Reel o' Tullochgorum" struck up, Fitzmuddle was so excited, whether by the melody, the whisky toddy, or the charms of the "sweet Highland girl," that he started up, and seizing Maggie by the hand actually reeled through the reel, and made an energetic if not altogether successful attempt to "shak' a fit," and fit the poetry of motion to that of music in the Highland fling; and when, after five minutes of the hardest gymnastic exercise he had ever gone through, he subsided into his chair, he pronounced it to be real good fun.

It is a curious thing how dancing develops the real type and true national spirit of different races. The Scotch reel illustrates to the life that "Perfervidum ingenium Scotorum," the glowing white heat in the inner furnace of a Scotchman's soul, which on rare occasions breaks through the outer surface of caution, shrewdness, and reserve, and gives us in the lower ranks of life a "Miller Rab," or a "Maggie Lauder," and in the higher a Burns, a Walter Scott, or a Gordon. Look again at an Italian, a Frenchman, and an Englishman, dancing a *pas seul* in a quadrille, or leading out a lady in a cotillon. The Italian does it with an easy spontaneous grace that makes the performance a pretty little artistic picture; the Frenchman looks like a little strutting bantam-cock who fancies himself the cynosure of the admiring eyes of a bevy of hens; while the true-born Briton simply looks and feels like a fool: either he stalks solemnly through his part, looking as if he were doing penance for some unutterable sin, or else, from the fear of looking so, he falls into the opposite extreme, and indulges in some grotesque and extravagant capers.

So with other nations: German men and maidens float round in the slow sentimental waltz, or at least did so, until their natural taste got sophisticated by the hoppy-jumpy waltzes which have supplanted the beautiful, melodious strains of Beethoven, Mozart, and Weber; while the Pole jingles his spurs in the polka, and shows the brilliant but ostentatious and inconsequent spirit which, in more important matters, has brought his country to grief.

However, the genuine Scotch national spirit reigned supreme at Fitzmuddle's ball, and even the grave and reverend seniors, who sat at the long table and stuck steadily to the whisky toddy, wagged their white beards and venerable heads, and beat time with their fists on the table and their feet below it, to the inspiring strains of MacAlister the piper.

But everything in this world comes to an end, and some of the lads and lasses had far to go, so towards midnight the party broke up, though not without drinking Fitzmuddle's health and long life to him, to which he responded in a speech which, although somewhat incoherent, fairly brought the house down when he concluded by saying, that for many a long day he should think of that night and sing :

My heart's in the Hielands, my heart is na here.

When they got out into the cool night air, it was dark, but the stars were out and shining brightly, and Fitzmuddle insisted on walking up the glen with Maggie to see her to her aunt's cottage. Maggie would have declined the honour, but glancing over her shoulder, she saw Donald still glooming and in the act of putting the shawl on Flora Fraser, and bidding her good-night. So the spirit of mischief seized her, and turning with a smile to Fitzmuddle, she told him that he might just gang a wee bit o' the way with her up the glen, to cool himself after the crowded room and whisky toddy.

Fitzmuddle in his sober senses was the most modest of mortals, and would as soon have thought of kissing the Queen, as of taking any liberty with the humblest female who ever wore a petticoat.   But to-night he had drank an extra glass of whisky toddy, and as Burns says :

> Wi' usquebaugh we fear nae evil,
> Wi' tippenny we'll face the devil.

And if the devil, how much more a comely lassie with whom we have been dancing and flirting all the evening ! Accordingly, when it came to wishing her good-night outside her aunt's cottage, Fitzmuddle's arm, straying from the paths of propriety, found itself encircling Maggie's capacious waist, while his lips whispered in her ear :

"Give a fellow a kiss, just one kiss, like a darling good girl."

The astonished Maggie uttered something between a skirl and a giggle, and said :

"Behave yourself, Mr. Fitzmuddle, and take your arm away, or I'll just gie you a good skelping, and send you home wi' a flea in your ear."

Whether Fitzmuddle would have proceeded to further extremities, and whether Maggie would have carried out her threat, are questions which must remain unsolved in the womb of time ; for even as the valiant knight Sir Tristram, bending his head to place warm kisses on the white neck of the fair Yseult, heard a sudden cry and felt a sudden blow; so in a second of time, Fitzmuddle found himself prostrate on the grass, with a thousand stars glancing in his eyes from a heavy blow on the forehead, administered by the strong arm of Donald Cameron, who, fired by jealous fury, had followed the couple up the glen. Picking himself up and regaining his feet, Fitzmuddle, with the innate gallantry of his distinguished race, faced the unequal contest, and throwing himself into an attitude inspired by his recollection of a sporting print of the battle between Tom Sayers and Heenan, squared boldly at his redoubtable antagonist. Donald, when his blood was up, cared not for man or devil, and drew back his right arm for another blow, which would probably have proved a finisher.

But as Athene on the "ringing plains of windy Troy" threw her broad ægis over her wounded

hero to protect him from the insulting foe, or
as the Sabine matron rushed with outstretched
arms between the sword of her father Tatius and
the spear of her husband Romulus, so Maggie
threw her capacious charms between Fitzmuddle
and his assailant, and seizing hold of the latter's
arm, exclaimed :

"Oh, Donald, dinna strike the puir laddie ;
dinna for my sake ; it's my fault and no his.
And you, sir, get your ways home as fast as you
can ; Donald's five times as strong as you, and
when he's mad, he's waur than any Hielan' bull."

Fitzmuddle, however bemuddled, had sense
enough left to recognise the soundness of this
advice, and accordingly commenced a rapid
strategical movement to the rear, which only
terminated when he found himself safely ensconced in the fortification of his feather bed
and double pair of blankets.

The gleam of the morning sun through the
bedroom window of the unfortunate Fitzmuddle
roused him from his sleep of stupor, and found
him perhaps the most miserable mortal in Her

Majesty's dominions. He had a racking headache, a dull pain between the eyes, and an uneasy consciousness that one, if not both of them,
was likely to wear for several days the sable
livery of mourning. But his bodily pains were
as nothing compared with his mental agonies.
As he gradually recalled the recollections of what
had occurred after he left the ball to walk home
with Maggie, his imagination depicted them in
the darkest colours. He had behaved like a
snob, had grossly insulted her, and had been
soundly and deservedly thrashed for doing so
by his own gamekeeper. How should he ever
look them in the face, or show himself outside
the door, with his tell-tale black eye exciting
the comments of the whole community? Utterly
wretched he lay, tossing on his bed for half-an-
hour, till at length his better nature asserted
itself, and he said: "Well, I have been a fool and
a snob, there is no use denying it; so there is
only one thing to be done, and that is to confess it like a man, make Maggie a humble apology
and ask Donald to forgive me."

It is wonderful what consolation there is in true repentance; in not trying to deceive yourself by illusions, or to get out of a scrape by a lie, but looking things fairly in the face, touching bottom, and coming to a firm determination to take whatever punishment may be in store for you bravely, and having sinned and suffered, to sin no more. Even worse scrapes than poor Fitzmuddle had got into, may, if met in this spirit, turn out to be blessings in disguise. Invigorated by this resolution, Fitzmuddle sprang out of bed, looked in the glass, and saw that one eye only was blackened, and that not so badly as he had feared, and after a tub of cold water, felt his head better, and going downstairs sat down to a cup of tea and slice of toast.

While thus engaged the servant-girl opened the door and said: "Please, sir, Maggie Macdonald is here, and would like to speak with you."

"Show her in, show her in at once," said Fitzmuddle, feeling like a man who, having a tooth to be drawn, is anxious to get it over as quickly as possible.

Maggie entered the room with some hesitation, and stood for a moment with her clear eyes cast down, and blushing red as a full-blown rose. She tried to speak, but the words seemed to stick in her throat, and she quite forgot the pretty speech she had composed, breaking down before she had got further than, " Oh, sir ; oh, Mr. Fitzmuddle ! "

But Fitzmuddle, jumping up from his chair, anticipated her. " Maggie," he said, " I know what you have come about. I behaved like a brute last night ; I have no excuse to make, and can only make you a humble apology and ask you to forgive me."

" Oh, sir," said Maggie, " you are too good, too good altogether. It's no for myself I am come to see you, but to plead for Donald. He was just mad last night, and if it came to the Factor's ears that he had struck your honour, he'd have his discharge that day, and he and his auld mother wad be turned out of their cot-house and warned off the estate."

" Tell the Factor, indeed ? " said Fitzmuddle.

"I just think not; do you take me for a sneak to do such a thing?"

"I maun just tell your honour the truth about me and Donald," said Maggie, "for it's the best excuse that can be made for him. He and I have been engaged to be married this twa years past."

"Dear me, dear me," said Fitzmuddle, "I had not the least idea of that. What a pity I did not know sooner, for I should have been ever so much more careful! I suppose he was jealous because I liked to talk and dance with you better than with any of the other lasses."

"'Deed, sir," said Maggie, "that's just the honest truth. Donald's a good lad, but he has a hot temper of his ain, and I was angry with him for misjudging me, and so carried on a bit too far just to vex him. But noo we've had it out and made it up, and oh, if your honour wad only forgie him it's happy we wad baith be."

"Forgive him?" said Fitzmuddle; "why, it's he who has to forgive me. I wish he were here this minute to tell him so."

His wish had not to wait for its fulfilment, for Maggie darted out of the room calling out: "Donald, come ben, I say, come ben this very instant," and returned, dragging Donald by the hand, who had been waiting outside for the result of her mission.

Donald looked rather sheepish and embarrassed, and stood twisting his Highland bonnet in his hands and shifting from one leg to the other. Fitzmuddle came straight up to him and said: "Donald, you knocked me down last night and gave me a black eye."

Donald gave a half-articulate grunt of assent, and cast an imploring glance on Maggie.

"And, Donald," proceeded Fitzmuddle, "I have thought the matter over and heard Maggie's story, and my private opinion is, you served me quite right; so I beg your pardon, and if you will forgive me this time, here is my hand; give me yours, and we will have a hearty shake and be fast friends for the future."

Donald's eyes filled with tears, his throat swelled, and his voice fairly broke, as he held forth his hand and stammered out:

"You're too guid—altogether too guid. Oh, sir—oh!" and here he fairly broke down; but Maggie interpreted for him and said:

"He means that you're a guid man and a true gentleman, and that he and I wad gae through fire and water for you, and sae we ought, for such kindness from a grand gentleman like you to puir bodies like us is past belief."

"Nay, Maggie," said Fitzmuddle, "one man's as good as another; and where was the grand gentleman, I wonder, when Donald there fished him out of the water with his gaff? And that reminds me that I promised to do him any favour he asked me for saving my life on that occasion. Have you nothing to ask for him, Maggie? Why don't you two get married off-hand? I'm sure Donald would be the better of you to look after him, and keep him from getting into passions and knocking people down."

Maggie replied: "You see, sir, Donald is sair set on going to America; he's got a proud spirit, and would fain go to a new country where a man has a chance to rise; and I wad fain gae

wi' him, but no to be a hindrance to him; and
his auld mither has to be provided for, and
his sister, that's Mistress Macrae, who the auld
woman wad gae to live with, is but puir, and
has bairns o' her ain, so she wad need £10
to keep her till we could send her money
from America; and the passage to New York
and railway to California, where Donald's bent
on going, wad come to £10 or £15 each to
do it respectable, so that makes £40, and we
wad need at the least £10 or £20 mair to keep
us till we could look about and find work; so
Donald and I just concluded to wait till we had
saved up £60 between us, and that takes a long
day, and if your honour had no been so guid
and had telled the factor, it wad hae been
longer still, and we should ha' been grey-headed
baith before we wan to America."

"Is that all?" said Fitzmuddle, with a cheery
laugh; "that is soon mended. Just set the favour
I promised Donald at £100; take that from me,
and we will cry quits, and go and tell the minister
to put your names up in the kirk next Sunday."

"I couldna do it," said Donald, "indeed I couldna; you're far ower kind; but to tak' a sum o' money like that from a gentleman is what I could never do."

"But I am not a gentleman," said Fitzmuddle, "but a friend, and I have plenty of money; and you cannot think how disappointed I should feel if you put me at arm's length with your confounded Highland pride and would not take anything from me."

And indeed the problem thus raised of taking or refusing a free gift freely offered, is one of the most delicate and difficult with which a man can have to deal. On the one hand, no doubt a man can hardly accept money without a shock to his pride, and some weakening of the feeling of self-respect which tells him that money is a thing which ought to be earned by his own exertions; and there is no more contemptible object than a man who, having once broken down this barrier of self-respect, sorns on his friends and relations, and finally sinks down to the level of a begging-letter writer. But, on the other hand, there are rare occasions on which more true nobility of nature is shown in accepting than in giving. To deny one's pride the pleasure of refusing, when the receiver is convinced that the donor can afford the gift, and will derive real pleasure from the acceptance, and real pain from the refusal, is a greater act of self-denial than to part with £100 which you do not miss. Above all, to accept freely and generously, one must have sufficient confidence in oneself to feel that you are really not lowering your moral standard, and doing an unworthy act for the sake of the money; and sufficient imagination to be able to transport yourself into the person of the donor, and feel that, if the positions were reversed, you would to a certainty act and feel as he does.

However, Maggie, without going into these intricate reasonings, with her true woman's feeling, and quick woman's wit, hit upon a solution which admirably reconciled the two opposite conclusions.

"Donald," she said, "you're partly right and partly wrong. I wadna hae ye take any man's money as a gift, not even his honour's ; but what Mr. Fitzmuddle says is true, and after what he has done for us it isna for us to vex him by refusing to let him help us. I am sure he means it, and it would vex him sair to think we were too proud to take help at his hands. And, Donald, a hundred pounds is a grand lot o' siller, and wad be the making of us in a new country ; suppose we say we'll take it as a loan, and I am sure we'll baith work our fingers to the bane to repay it, if our lives be spared."

"I had far rather you would take it and say nothing about loans," said Fitzmuddle.

"Na, na, sir," said Donald. "Maggie's just right; and if you'll mak' it a loan, Donald Cameron will no taste whisky or smoke tobacco till it's repaid ; and we'll baith be mair beholden to you than if you had given us a thousand pounds in a present."

"Well, well," said Fitzmuddle, "I suppose wilful folk maun hae their way, as your Scotch proverb has it, so a loan be it, though mind, you are to be in no hurry about repaying it ; and as to stopping your baccy, I could not be happy to think of it; I should never enjoy a cigar again if I thought of you pulling at an empty pipe after a hard day's work; so let us compound for the whisky, and allow even an odd drop of that if you get Maggie's leave for it. And so that job is finished; you will find the £100 at your credit in the National Bank; and now good-bye, for I've got to pack up my traps and be off early in the morning by the steamer."

"May the Lord reward you," said Maggie and Donald simultaneously, "for we canna. May every gude blessing be with you as you have brought one on us. Oh, sir, we canna find words to thank you."

"Nonsense," said Fitzmuddle, "you will make me cry if you go on like that; and now, Maggie, I asked you for a kiss last night, and I am going to ask you again, but not for one that will make Donald jealous. Give me your hand, my dear, good, bonnie lass."

Maggie held out her hand, and large as it was, like a well-shaped man's hand, and red with the frequent labours of the washing-tub, Fitz-muddle bent over it and kissed it with as much stately courtesy as if it had been the white be-jewelled hand of a duchess.

Next morning he was off to seek the "fresh fields and pastures new" of Leicestershire; but, early as it was, a crowd had assembled at the pier, and there was cheering and waving of handkerchiefs till the steamer rounded the point, and one couple stood hand in hand at the end of the pier, with tears in their eyes, and grateful blessings in their hearts for the generous benefactor who had so unexpectedly smoothed the path of their young lives, and started them, loving and hopeful, to seek their fortunes in a new world. Of those fortunes some glimpse may be afforded before this history comes to a conclusion; but for the present it is enough to say that at the end of twelve months a re-mittance of £25 was sent through the Bank of California from one Donald Cameron, £10 for his old mother, and £15 to the credit of the Honourable Augustus Fitzmuddle; and before

two years had elapsed the whole debt was repaid, and Donald was free to smoke unlimited
tobacco and to drink as much whisky as his
prudent better-half thought was necessary for the
good of his constitution.

CHAPTER VIII.

FITZMUDDLE IN THE SHIRES—FOX-HUNTING.

THE scene now changes from the mountains of Mull to the rich pastures of Leicestershire, where Fitzmuddle is about to learn his first lessons in the noble science of the chase.

Why is fox-hunting rightly called the king of sports ?

I have meditated deeply on this momentous question, and seen the thing as it really is, with the eyes of practical experience. For, reader, I too have

> Drunk delight of battle with my peers,

and seen a good many

> Fast thirty minutes from Ranksborough Gorse.

Ay, and jumped not a few oxers, and brushed

through bullfinches, and charged brooks—not quite
so wide or high as one sees in sporting prints, and
reads of in sporting novels, and possibly not quite
so wide or high as they seemed to myself, when
I sat with a glass of good claret before me and
my legs under the mahogany—but still quite wide
and high enough to bring my heart into my
mouth when I crammed my hat down and put
my horse at them. And though I never rode
quite in the first flight, I rode near enough to it
to see what hunting was like to those who kept
within sight of the flying pack as it swept, like
the shadow of a cloud on a breezy day, over the
wide pastures of Leicestershire.

And this is the result of my experience :

In the first place, fox-hunting is a grand sport,
because it tests what is the foundation of most
of the real worth of a man—physical courage.

There is no very great amount of courage
required to shoot at a grouse or pheasant, who
can't shoot back at you in return ; or even to
pot a noble stag from behind a boulder or a
peat-hag. And as for fishing, why, Byron's wish

is seldom realised, that the fish and the man should change places, and the latter should

> In his gullet,
> Have a sharp hook, and a small trout to pull it ;

though, by-the-bye, how much more genial would Byron's poetry have been, if, like dear old Isaac Walton, he had loved to stray on a summer's morning across the flowery meadows, and meet milkmaids, fresh and blooming as the cowslips, and send them home happy with a shilling to buy blue ribbons to "tie up their bonny brown hair " !

And there is another object of the too frequent chase of the coarser sort of man—poor helpless woman, who cannot retort against any insult or injury with any sharper weapon than her tongue, and her meek pathetic eyes ; and the man who is brute enough to insult a woman is not likely to mind these much.

But in fox-hunting it is quite different ; and a stiff post and rail, or high wattled hedge with treacherous ditch on the far side, and a bad take-off out of plough, do most effectually and unmistakably resent any injudicious familiarities. And, take my word for it, if you do not possess some fair share of that primary attribute of manhood, physical courage, you had better stay at home, or confine your hunting to MacAdam and the mahogany. But granted this primary attribute, it is only the foundation on which to build up the edifice of the reputation of a man "who rides well to hounds."

When Sir Joshua Reynolds was asked what he mixed his colours with to produce such brilliant results, he replied : " Sir, I mix them with brains."

So it is with most things in this world, and with fox-hunting among others. For the man who aspires to be one of those whose familiar face is generally to be seen among the favoured twenty or thirty, out of a field of two or three hundred, who are mopping their faces, and looking at their watches, and loosening their horses' girths, after a sharp thirty or forty minutes' burst over a stiff country, where fences are big and come often, must unite discretion with valour. His wits must never be wool-gathering. He must have brain-power enough to fix his attention on what he is about, and not be mooning on the wrong side of the covert when the hounds get away ; or, if he does get a fair start, he must keep his wits about him, and be constantly watching how the leading hounds turn, or if they run so fast that he cannot quite see the hounds, he must try to watch the huntsman, or the coat-tails of some of the foremost riders as they disappear before him over the fences. And, above all, he must have quick decision, and make up his mind in a moment when he gets into a field how he means to get out of it ; and if he comes to an extra high fence or wide brook, whether he means to have it or not, or if not, then he must gallop off at once for the nearest bridle-gate or ford.

But the chosen one or two who do habitually cut out the work and go foremost, not on paper only, must have these qualities in a superlative degree. They must have nerves of iron, and, like Nelson, have to ask what fear is like, for they have never felt it. And their decision must be like that of Frederick the Great's famous Hussar, General Von Seidletz, who, when he was riding with his master one day across a bridge, and Frederick asked him in jest what he would do if a Russian picket appeared at the far end, and a squadron of Austrians closed up the end behind them, for sole answer wheeled his horse round, jumped him over the low parapet into the river, and swam to the shore. And an eye for country they must have, like the eagle glance with which Wellington detected the false move of Marmont, when he sent Foy down from the hill of the Arapiles to spread his division out and try to turn the English left, and our Iron Duke met him with a swift swoop, as of a falcon's wing, and sent Marmont and his 60,000 veterans running for dear life from Salamanca to Burgos.

Now these are exceptional gifts, and he who has them is a born leader of men; and the beauty of fox-hunting is that it puts all ranks on a level, and it is the *man* and not the title or money-bags that come to the front. I have seen a young farmer on a broken-kneed gray mare, that did not look worth a £20 note, cutting out the work for peers and baronets on their 300-guinea steeds; and I have seen a butcher's boy on a ragged pony wriggle through bullfinches, and scramble down one side of wide ditches and up the other, when the most stupendous swells, got up with the perfection of new red coats, and boots, and leathers, drew rein, and craned their necks, and waited for some one else to go first—though the swell was always first over after dinner.

Moreover, there is one great requisite of good riding, and that is to have what are called "good hands." And good hands are essentially a question of good temper, and of regard and sympathy for the noble animal who strains every sinew to carry you to the front if you will only let him. You must never be angry and jerk his mouth, or careless, and pull him up sharp with the curb; but always be on the give and take with him, and trying to humour him, and get to talk in a friendly, rational way with him through the bit, which is the poor horse's almost only means of establishing communication between you and him. This is probably the reason why ladies, as a rule, have so much better hands than men.

It is not only the fine nervous wrist that does it, but the finer sympathy ; for ladies are almost always fonder of their horses than men ; and love gets its return with a high rate of interest, in sympathy and a better understanding almost everywhere where it is invested. So fox-hunting has more in it than meets the eye, and is really one of the best cramming schools for a competitive examination in many of the finest qualities.

If so many of our golden youth, with all their faults and follies, are manly, high-spirited fellows, ready to lead their men, and the men ready to follow them, when the Russian masses are surging up the heights of Inkermann, or the dusky Arabs swarming in with sword and spear, when the angle of the square has been broken at Tamanieb or Abu-Klea, it is very much owing to fox-hunting. If they are, as we fondly hope, less luxurious and effeminate than those of their class in other countries, is it not in a great measure owing to that little animal the fox; and would they have

been what they are if their chases had been confined
to those of pretty faces and neat ankles, and their
decision to that of staking on red or black when
the croupier drones out his monotonous cry of
" Faites votre jeu, Messieurs " ?

Therefore it is no wonder that in hunting
counties the fox is worshipped as a sacred animal,
and to kill one, otherwise than in fair sport, is
thought to be a considerably worse crime than
killing a Christian.

For the enjoyment of this noble sport Fitzmuddle had, as we have seen, made his preliminary
preparations with due care and deliberation.
Martingale had really got together a very fair
stud of hunters.

First there was Sobersides, a big brown horse,
who was a perfect model of propriety and decorum
of demeanour ; as slow as a top, he was as steady
as Stonewall Jackson's ranks at the battle of
Bull's Run. He never by any chance committed a
mistake, and negotiated all his fences with deliberation, but absolute safety. In short, he was
a perfect horse for a novice to ride whose ambition

was not so much to show in the first rank, as to learn the art of sticking on while jumping moderate fences.

Logician, a bright bay with a white star, was a different sort of animal. He had a fair turn of speed, and was an accomplished hunter at all sorts of fences, except timber, which he was rather apt to rush at and take carelessly; for, being a knowing sort of horse, he had found by experience that top rails are not always as strong as they look, and it is often less trouble to snap one in two than to jump over it. In fact, if he had a fault, it was that of being too knowing, and consequently too opinionative and fond of having his own way. As Martingale said of him : " He is that artful, that, if he could but speak, he would argue the head off your shoulders as well as any lawyer who ever wore a wig." But give him his own way, and, in nine cases out of ten, that way would be the right one, and he would carry you safely and easily in a good place through a good run.

The chestnut mare, Coquette, was the beauty

of the party. Clean thorough-bred, she was a picture to look at, with her glossy satin skin of golden chestnut, and her delicate little ears and silky mane and tail, and generally aristocratic and high-bred appearance. Fitzmuddle was never tired of looking at her and admiring her, as a high-born young lady in her first season might admire the beautiful ball dress in which she is to make her *début* at Court; and, as the vanity of personal appearance is not a commodity of which the female sex have by any means a monopoly, the idea did occasionally flit across his mind of what a pretty picture the Honourable Augustus Fitzmuddle would make, arrayed in a faultless red coat and immaculate tops and breeches, and mounted on this lovely mare.

The fourth horse, Velocipede, was a great raking chestnut, over sixteen hands high, and standing over a deal of ground, whom Martingale had been induced to buy at Lord Scattercash's sale in consequence of a tip he had received from his lordship's head groom, who was an old friend of his, that the horse had been tried good enough to win a big steeple-chase, and that if my lord had not come to grief at Ascot, and been obliged to send everything to the hammer, he believed they would have entered him for the Grand National. Martingale could not resist the seduction of possibly winning some good hunt race, and, as the horse was entirely dark, getting long odds and winning a pot of money; so although a potential steeple-chaser was not exactly the mount for a beginner, he compounded with his conscience by resolving to spare no pains in teaching his master to ride.

Being well known in the Shires, and popular with the farmers, from whom he often bought hay and corn, he made friends with one young sporting farmer about two miles from Belton, who had a grass farm with a good many tolerably easy fences which, with the aid of a few gorsed hurdles, and a little backing up, made a very respectable training-ground, in which to take preparatory gallops. Having bought his hay from this farmer, and promised to put him on the first real good thing he knew of in the racing way, he readily obtained permission to use this private course as much as he liked. Accordingly he first proceeded to train his master's horses over it, and then to train his master himself.

For Fitzmuddle, on leaving Mull, had followed Martingale's advice, and come straight to Reynard Lodge, so as to have a fortnight's schooling in the art of equitation, before putting in a first appearance at the opening meet.

It would be absurd to say that in this short space of time he became an accomplished, or even a tolerable horseman ; and, as the record of his experiences will show, he had much to go through before acquiring any decent proficiency in the art. Still it is wonderful how much a man may learn in a short time, on two conditions—first, that he is not afraid of tumbling off, and secondly, that he gives his whole mind to it. Fitzmuddle complied with both these requisites, for his pluck was undeniable, and he was most anxious to learn, and devoted several hours every day to schooling himself under Martingale's tuition over Farmer Day's fences. At the first attempt he was shot

over his horse's head; at the next he was only
shot on to his neck, and very nearly preserved his
balance; at the third he was shot only half-way
along the neck, and managed to scramble back
into the saddle; and so on until, after five or six
attempts, though a good deal of daylight might
be seen between him and the saddle, he generally
came down within a few inches of where he had
taken off from the saddle, and by the end of a
fortnight he could stick on over a hurdle or
straightforward hedge or ditch, not altogether
ingloriously. Two things conspired to give him
confidence; first, that he found by experience that
tumbling off was not such a dreadful thing after
all, for, with an average of two or three falls a day,
he never hurt himself; the other was that it was
so much easier to take a good-sized fence at a fly,
going boldly at it at a good pace, than to boggle
at a stand over one of less formidable dimensions.

However, jumping easy fences in a riding-
school or training-ground, is a very different thing
from taking the obstacles, good, bad, and indifferent, as they occur in practice in the hunting-

field, as Fitzmuddle soon found; and before arriving at the goal of his ambition of riding fairly well to hounds, he had to go through a good many experiences, some of which we will proceed to relate.

It happened singularly enough that these early experiences resolved themselves into lessons, not only in the art of riding, but in the weightier and more abstruse subjects of mechanics and natural philosophy.

His first appearance was at the opening meet. Martingale sagely advised that he should stick to Sobersides on this first occasion; but, as we hinted, Fitzmuddle's fancy had been so excited by the picture in his mind's eye of his appearance on the charming Coquette, that he pleaded to be allowed to ride her. The matter was at length compromised by arranging that Fitzmuddle should ride Coquette to the meet, which was only three miles off, and when the hounds threw off he should exchange for Sobersides, whom Martingale would ride on.

On one point, however, he accepted Martingale's advice, viz., to make his first appearance in a black coat; for, as Martingale said, "If a gent sport a red coat, it is a sort of advertisement to the world that he means to ride; and nothing looks so bad as to see a swell in pink not taking his fences in his turn, but craning, or turning away, and going with a lot of outsiders in search of gates and gaps ; but if a man is in a black coat no one particularly notices him."

Accordingly, in a neat-fitting black coat, but with unexceptionable boots and breeches, our hero mounted the beautiful Coquette and rode her slowly on to the meet.

The opening meet was at Kingsley Hall, a fine mansion with an Italian portico, in a large and well-timbered park, from which the grounds were separated by a low ha-ha fence. The hounds were clustered round the huntsman just outside the fence, and more than three hundred gallant sportsmen were collected, a large proportion of them in red coats, with a number of ladies in their neatest and best-fitting habits; while a large array of farmers, boys on ponies, and miscellaneous roughs and rustics, the latter drawn there partly by the attractions of the chase and partly by those of the bread and cheese and ale which were liberally served out, added to the animation of the scene.

The *habitués* of the hunt were mostly inside the fence, and many of them dismounted, to the great satisfaction of the men who held their horses, and entered the hall, where they fortified the inner man, and steadied their nerves for the coming run, by glasses of sherry and nips of cherry brandy and Curaçoa.

But Fitzmuddle remained outside, partly from the innate modesty of his nature, and partly, to tell the truth, because Coquette, though generally as good as she was beautiful, showed some slight symptoms of excitement at seeing such a crowd, and once or twice laid back her ears and switched her tail in a somewhat ominous manner. Fitzmuddle, therefore, took up what he considered to be a safe post of observation away from the crowd, and close to a nursery-maid with a perambulator, who was watching the proceedings with great interest from a point as near the hounds and huntsmen as she could venture to go. He watched the speckled beauties with intense delight, and edged a little nearer to them; when, unfortunately, one of the pack, Mischief by name, made a little excursion in the direction of Coquette's heels. The quick eye of the first whip detected the departure from discipline in a moment, and the crack of his whip, resounding like a pistol-shot, elicited a loud yell from the truant hound and recalled her to a sense of duty. But, unfortunately also for Fitzmuddle, it acted also as the last straw which broke the camel's back of Coquette's suppressed excitement, and, with a sudden squeal, she bucked high in the air and flung out her heels still higher. To sit a horse who suddenly combines the operations of bucking and kicking requires a good rider, who is not sitting loosely and thinking of something else. In Fitzmuddle's case both these requisites were wanting. A good rider he certainly was not yet, whatever he might become; and his thoughts happened to be wandering in another direction—let us charitably hope not that in which a pair of pretty eyes were looking from under the nurse-maid's sunshade. Anyhow, the result was that he was projected obliquely upwards; and if he had been asked in a competitive examination to draw the curve in which a heavy body under such circumstances falls to the ground by the force of gravity, he would have got full marks, for he could not have described a prettier parabola.

A parabola fortunately, and not an ellipse; for, had the initial velocity been somewhat greater, he would have been shot into space, as some astronomers say the moon was at some early period of the earth's history, and would at this moment have been revolving in a planetary orbit as a second satellite intermediate between the earth and the moon.

Fortunately no such catastrophe happened, and his connection with mother earth was not thus abruptly severed; his parabolic descent ending at the feet of the pretty nurse-maid, and narrowly escaping coming, comet-like, into fatal collision with her infant charge in the perambulator.

The nurse-maid screamed, the roughs and rustics guffawed, and the more polished assembly, with smiles and sneers, asked one another who this muff was who had come out to air his horsemanship with the crack Thorn pack at their crack meet on the opening day. Sundry small jokes passed as to his being a tailor intent on cutting out the work, or an organist who had selected that occasion to practise voluntaries.

Fitzmuddle ruefully picked himself up, none the worse for his tumble, but decidedly a wiser and a sadder man; and on Martingale's coming up with Sobersides, he made no further objection to exchanging the brilliant Coquette for that safer and steadier conveyance.

Mounted on that sedate animal he felt much more at his ease, and when the hounds found in the laurels that bounded one side of the park, he went away with them and jumped five or six fences; and, though they soon ran him out of sight, he followed with the ruck in the rear through gates and gaps; and as the fox after a twenty minutes' burst ran into a drain, he got up in time to see him bolted and killed, and thus could truly aver that he had been in at the death. So he jogged home, not altogether dissatisfied with his first essay, notwithstanding that initial misadventure.

Fitzmuddle's next lesson in mechanical science occurred in the following manner. After his first essay on the opening day, he practised assiduously, and improved so rapidly that Martingale pronounced him quite equal to the feat of riding Logician.

"You have only to let him have his own way, sir," he said, "and you will find him quite easy to ride, and he will carry you well in front, and give you no trouble but to sit still and stick on."

Accordingly, when the hounds found and went away from Handley Wood, Fitzmuddle, who got a good start, went on for a time delightfully. The line was over large grass fields with moderate fences, until at last they came to one, the boundary of which was a post and rail, not particularly high or strong, but enough to turn a good many away;

for it is wonderful how many dislike the look of timber, and, though they would jump a hurdle, are afraid of a post and rail, which is no higher.

But there was one who was not afraid of it, and that was Mr. Heavystern, who came up to it just before Fitzmuddle, and about twenty yards to his left.

Mr. Heavystern was a well-known farmer in these parts, who exemplified admirably that pre-established harmony of things which has ordained that

Who drive fat oxen should themselves be fat,

for he was heavy in name, heavy in person, he rode a heavy horse, and he farmed heavy acres. He weighed at least twenty stone, and was broad of beam as a Dutch galliot. He might have been called bullet-headed, only his head was rather of the dimensions of a cannon-ball, and with his close-cropped black hair, blue stubbly beard, little pig eyes and huge cheeks, might have been carved out of one of those gigantic turnips which are commemorated in provincial newspapers. His horse was a great raw-boned black with a rat tail, who looked like a brewer's dray-horse, from whose ribs all the fat had been melted off by carrying the welter weight of his rider. But huge of bulk and uncouth as they were, Heavystern and his horse were often seen well in front in a run, for the farmer was undeniably a hard man, and could crash by sheer momentum through almost any fence in Leicestershire, while he knew every gap and bridle-gate and short cut for miles round.

Thus it happened that he came to the post and rail just before Fitzmuddle, and galloped straight through it, making it fly in splinters as if it had been a cobweb. When Fitzmuddle saw the gap he tried to pull Logician towards it, but he might just as well have pulled at a stone wall. Whether this attempt to interfere with him put Logician out, or whether seeing the top-rail give way so easily before Heavystern's charge led him for once to make a miscalculation, and think it would be less trouble to smash it than to jump it, I am unable to say, but the result was, that when he struck it with his knees it did not give way, but turned him right over

into the next field. Had Fitzmuddle been a better
rider and stuck to the saddle, the consequences
might have been serious, but having a loose seat,
he was shot far enough clear of his horse, and
they both picked themselves up none the worse
for the mishap. By the time he had caught his
horse and mounted, the hounds had run out of
sight, and he would have seen nothing more of
them had they not, after running another mile,
thrown up their heads and come to a long check
in a ploughed field, which happened to be on
Mr. Heavystern's farm. They cast round and
round, and backwards and forwards, with no
result; and the field had mostly drawn up to
the bridle-gate at its far corner to be ready for
a fresh start, when Fitzmuddle overtook them.
Mr. Heavystern was standing a little back from
the rest, still watching some hounds who were
puzzling along the edge on the far side.

When Logician saw him it is evident that the
sagacious animal had worked out in his head the
problem set him by what had occurred at the post
and rail, and arrived at the conclusion that, as

momentum equals weight multiplied by velocity, the way to make up for deficiency in the former factor was to increase the latter. Accordingly he seized the bit between his teeth, put on his very best pace, and charged Mr. Heavystern and his horse, who were standing broadside on, with such velocity, that he sent man and horse rolling over and over. As the Templar in the lists of Ashby-de-la-Zouch rolled over before the lance of Ivanhoe three times, grasping the grass and sand each time, so did Heavystern on this occasion, grasping handfuls of his own clay. And when at last he ceased rolling, and sat on his own broad stern on his own broad acres, another still more interesting fact in natural philosophy was beautifully illustrated. The "correlation of force," as it is called, teaches us that all the energies of the universe are indestructible, and simply appear, Proteus-like, under different forms and transformations. Thus, in the present case, the mechanical force, which had been expended in the collision, reappeared in an exact equivalent of heat and energy (of language).

Double-barrelled oaths jostled one another with amazing adjectives at such a rate from Heavy-stern's mouth, that Fitzmuddle was only too glad when Melody hit off the scent by the hedge-row in the field beyond, and there was a rush for the bridle-gate, under cover of which he escaped from the vengeance of the infuriated farmer.

Fitzmuddle's exhibition on the lawn of Kings-ley Hall on the opening day, and the rumours which did not fail to be circulated as to his colli-sion with Mr. Heavystern, naturally caused a good deal of merriment among the swells of the hunt, and although he improved so rapidly that he was some-times in front of some of those who laughed most loudly at his expense, yet when a man once gets the character of being a muff in the hunting-field it is not so easy to shake it off.   It must be admitted also that in his inexperience he occasionally did things which could hardly fail to provoke a smile from the good-natured, and a sneer from the ill-natured spectator.

Thus, one day when the hounds came to a long check on the bank of the famous Missenden brook, Fitzmuddle, who was standing near a bridge across it, espied an excited rustic in a smock-frock, who, pointing with a dung-fork towards a little copse about a mile off, exclaimed :

"I zeed un; fox be gone that way for Boodler's Copse."

Fitzmuddle thought he would do an exceedingly clever thing by galloping off at once for the copse, and so getting a good start of the field and the hounds. So, giving Coquette a touch with his heel, he set off at a racing pace across the bridge and up the next field, rising in his stirrups and squaring his elbows, under the impression that he was showing the lookers-on a pretty exact imitation of Fred Archer or Charley Wood riding a Derby favourite in its preliminary canter. This attracted the attention of Captain Hardup, late of the Buffers, a well-known member of the hunt, whose income generally showed a negative figure, the positive side being represented by debts, I.O.U.'s, and overdue bills; and whose principal means of eking it out consisted in being "hail fellow well met" with all the young swells, getting asked to their dinners and winning their money by bets or at loo. Turning to Sir Samuel Simpleton, who happened to be next him, the gallant captain said :

"Look at that fellow, Fitzmuddle, what a hurry he is in to discount a cheque (check) on a Leicestershire Bank ; no wonder, when he is so confoundedly out at elbows."

Whereupon Simpleton laughed and said to himself : "What a deuced clever fellow Hardup is, to be sure ; he is quite one of the right sort." And he had occasion to think him still cleverer the next night, when they met at dinner at Lord Rattlebone's, and Hardup won £80 from him at loo in the course of the evening, and booked him for a bet of £100 to £25 against a horse who was scratched next week for the Grand National.

But the captain did not in the long run, as we shall see by-and-by, get much change out of Fitzmuddle.

Fitzmuddle's course of instruction in Natural

Philosophy was, however, not yet completed. His next experience taught a valauble lesson in the Chemistry of Organic Bodies, and the phenomena of their different molecular constitutions. In the beginning of December there was an early fall of snow, followed by a sharp frost, which for several days stopped hunting. At length a thaw came, and although the snow lay on the hill-tops and on the north side of the hedges, and the brooks were filled to the brim with melting snow-water, the hounds met at Bilton Wood. They soon found a fox, and as often happens after snow and frost, when the fields have been washed clean, there was a burning scent. The hounds ran at a great pace across the wide pastures towards Missenden, and Fitzmuddle, who was mounted on Logician, had nothing to do but let him take his own way and stick on as he best could, as he threw fence after fence behind him, and pulled his way very fairly towards the front. He enjoyed it thoroughly, and was in a glow of excitement and perspiration in spite of the raw and chilly air, when an ominous line of polled willows appeared in the middle of a wide grass field. There was no mistake about it, they were approaching the famous Missenden brook, in which so many saddles, stirrup-irons, hunting-crops, and flasks are said to be engulphed, that it has been seriously proposed to form a Joint-Stock Company for the purpose of dredging the brook for the salvage.

The hounds disappeared in it, and emerged one by one with dripping sterns, and immediately took up the scent and began to run harder than ever. There was not a bridge or ford to be seen, and evidently those who wished to see any more of the run, had to harden their hearts and trust to Providence to find an easy place to jump the brook. Even if he had been inclined to shirk it, Fitzmuddle knew very well that the decision lay not with him, but with Logician, and to do him justice, he was not at all disposed to turn tail in the middle of a good run, for fear of a fall or a ducking. So he thought of the exploits of the Squire and Captain Ross, over this same world-renowned brook, and, sticking his knees into the saddle as tight as he could, he never tried to stop

Logician, but let him race down at the brook at his own pace.

Now if he had been mounted on any other of his horses, he would probably have escaped without any mishap, for Coquette would have skimmed over it like a bird, Velocipede would have taken it in his stride, and Sobersides would have lobbed down to the bank, looked at it, and declined further acquaintance. But Logician took an intermediate course, for he came down fast to it, stopped for a single second to make a short mental calculation of its width and depth, and then, with a mighty bound, threw himself over and just reached the opposite bank. But that single second proved fatal to Fitzmuddle, for he was projected clean over the head of his horse, and fell with a mighty plump and splash into the very middle of the brook. It was out of his depth, but fortunately the branch of an old willow-tree hung over the stream, and before he had been carried many yards down, he caught hold of it and scrambled out on the bank. But unfortunately on the wrong side, and when he got the muddy water out of his eyes, he had the pleasure of seeing his horse careering gaily over the next field, with the dark, deep stream between them.

Now for the lesson to be derived from this experience. There is nothing which requires more caution in scientific experiments than to beware of being too hasty in assuming that apparently like causes will always produce like effects. It is a well-established fact that the immersion of red-hot iron in ice-cold water improves its temper, and converts the plebeian metal into aristocratic steel. Surely a similar effect may be expected to ensue from the molecular changes induced in other bodies by the same process. But, strange to say, the effect on the human body of plunging it suddenly, when at a glowing heat, in water of the temperature of melting snow, is not only not the same as in the case of metals, but, on the contrary, is precisely the reverse. Instead of improving the temper it makes it decidedly very much worse. Such at any rate was Fitzmuddle's experience; for, sweet-tempered as he generally was, I am obliged to confess that he felt uncommonly cross, and gave utterance to something very like profane ejaculations, as he trudged, wet to the skin and chilled to the marrow, across the fields, steering for the steeple of Missenden village, and he hardly recovered his composure until he gained the hospitable shelter of the "Fox and Hounds," got a dry suit of clothes from the landlord, and warmed himself thoroughly before a roaring fire, with a dish of fried eggs and bacon on the table and a glass of steaming hot brandy and water. After this, he ordered a fly, and, on arriving at Reynard Lodge, found that Logician had been brought back before him all right by a second horseman, whom he rewarded with half-a-sovereign.

As the season advanced, Fitzmuddle made such progress in his riding, that Martingale, who had watched him closely, said to him one day: "I really think, sir, you might begin to sport a red coat, you can ride as well as half the men who do, and have more pluck than nine-tenths of them; and after all the pink is the correct thing for a hunting gent." Fitzmuddle did not hesitate a moment in availing himself of Martingale's *imprimatur* to sport a brand-new red coat, which he had often gazed at hanging in his wardrobe with admiring eyes. For man is after all a vain creature, and it is very much the effect of habit and high civilisation that he does not constantly break out into gorgeous effulgencies of costume, as his Palæolithic ancestors did into tattooings and gaudy stripes of red and blue paint. And a red coat is a pardonable vanity, for a man in correct hunting costume does not look affected or coxcombical, but, on the contrary, more manly and gentlemanlike than in a pot hat and slovenly shooting-coat. And to a certain extent it is, or ought to be, a guarantee for a fair amount of physical courage in facing fences, and the sprinkling of scarlet gives life and animation to the scene, and pleases the children and rustics.

So I am altogether in favour of the devotees of the noble science of fox-hunting appearing in the correct costume of their sect at all its high rites and ceremonies, which, being interpreted, means when cub-hunting is over and regular meets begin.

But Fitzmuddle's first appearance in scarlet was very near being the occasion of a sad catastrophe. The hounds were running fast over the wide pastures beyond Sloughton-on-the-hill, and Fitzmuddle was holding a really creditable place, and striding along at a great pace across a forty-acre grass field, when his horse put his foot in a grip and down he came. The horse got up none the worse, and galloped off; but Fitzmuddle, though not hurt, was a little stunned and confused, and it took him a few seconds before he scrambled on to his legs and took in the situation. When he did so he saw a sight which might well appal the stoutest nerves.

There were cattle in the field, not the sober shorthorn or pacific pale-faced Herefords, who are generally met with in these parts, but, as ill-luck would have it, the farmer had just bought a herd of Irish bullocks and turned them into this field. Excited by the sight of the hounds running and horses galloping, these wild Irishmen were careering about the field, with heads and tails erect, making mad rushes in various directions.

Now, whether these particular bullocks were descendants of that famous bull who split a whole county into two factions, and set them flourishing shillelaghs and cracking crowns at every fair and market, on the question whether he was a four or five-year-old ; or were they simply nationalist bullocks who had been worked up to a pitch of fury by the impassioned harangues of a Healy or a Harrington, I cannot say. But more probably they had been listening to the singing of the "Wearing of the Green" until they had imbibed a hearty hatred for "England's cruel red." For certain it is that when they saw the brilliant red spot of Fitzmuddle's new coat in the middle of the green field, they charged straight down for it, like that

> Deluge of the foaming cavalry,

which, in Shelley's poem, was flung back from the steadfast square of the Greek patriots, or like Byron's

> Wolves who headlong go
> On the wounded buffalo.

But Fitzmuddle neither stood fast like Craig Ellachie's firm crag, nor like Scott's Fitzjames exclaimed :

> Come one, come all, this rock shall fly
> From its firm base, as soon as I ;

but rather like the English hero at the assault of Ismail in Byron's "Don Juan," took to that

> Running
> Which was a valorous sort of cunning.

And running he made for the nearest gate at his very best pace, which was by no means a bad one, for he was light of body and long of limb, and fear adds wings to flight, with twenty raging bullocks thundering in the rear.

Fast as he ran, however, the bullocks ran faster, and they would surely have overtaken him had not the leader, a huge, shaggy, black, long-horned animal, paused for a moment to vent his vengeance on Fitzmuddle's hat, which had come off and broken the guard-string when he fell. Even with this advantage they were close upon him before he reached the gate, and when he turned his head for a second, he could almost feel their hot breath on his cheek. However, with a last desperate spurt, he just managed to reach the gate, fortunately a high and strong five-barred one, and, tumbling over it, fell exhausted on the grass with the wind fairly pumped out of him. The bullocks, baulked of their vengeance on the base and brutal Saxon, were brought to a sudden stand, even as I have seen the full stream of Hibernian oratory suddenly arrested, when the Speaker's form, rising in all the dignity of flowing robe and full-bottomed wig, utters in accents impassive as fate, and stern as Rhadamanthus, the awful words: "Mr. O'Blather, member for Bally-buncum, I name you as trespassing on the time of the House and disregarding the authority of the Chair."

Fitzmuddle, as he lay panting for breath in his haven of safety, had thus his ideas of sport considerably enlarged by having occasion to contemplate it from the two opposite points of view of hunting and being hunted.

Hunting and being hunted, such is the universal and inexorable law of creation.

The fox they were pursuing had the day before gobbled up a harmless hen. But was the hen really so harmless when she gobbled up that busy little ant who was performing its duty as a good citizen in carrying home a captive aphide for the general advantage of the ant community? And so through all creation, life lives on life, the strong prey on the weak, the weak on the weaker, and down to the very lowest orders of being.

> Big fleas have little fleas upon their backs to bite 'em,
> And little fleas have lesser fleas, and so *ad infinitum.*

Nay, even the Brahmin, whose rule it is to destroy no living thing, is shocked, on looking through the microscope, to discover what legions of life he consumes in every draught of water. For, if there be any truth in the doctrine of the transmigration of souls, how can he tell that he may not thus be unwittingly swallowing down some venerable grand-aunt, or tough old grand-uncle, who for their sins in this world have been condemned to commence life anew at the bottom of the class, and in the lowest order of animated creation?

But the higher we rise in the scale, the keener becomes the chase, and the greater the contrast between the few who hunt and the many who are hunted. Who, in fact, are the heroes of the world's history? The Nimrods, Alexanders, Cæsars, Attilas, Napoleons, who are mighty hunters before the Lord, whose game is man, and who hunt down and slaughter their victims by millions. But at last comes the mightiest of all hunters, Death, who hunts down all alike, hunters and hunted, tyrants and slaves, oppressors and victims. His bag, when we come to think of it, is truly an enormous one. There are approximately some 1,200 millions of human beings living in this tiny planet, and three generations per century. Death, therefore, bags some 3,600 millions of the human species every century, and has been doing so, more or less, for the last fifty or sixty centuries, to say nothing of endless prehistoric barbarians and Palæolithic savages. And of these a small proportion only have lived out their full natural life, and attained to the Scriptural age of three-score and ten ; while a very large proportion, not less than twenty per cent., or 720 millions in each century, have died before they attained to anything like clear consciousness or conscience. Why were they born, why did they die, what were they before birth, what will they be after death ? Or are they simply Nature's failures and cast as "rubbish to the void"? And if so, is " love " really

> Creation's final law,

though

> Nature red in tooth and claw,
> With ravine shrieks against the creed.

Mystery of mysteries! What can we do but struggle, however faintly, with the poet, to hold on to some shred of the " larger hope " and feel that whatever may be

> Behind the veil,

our truest course is

> Because right is right to follow right,
> Were wisdom in the scorn of consequence.

Fitzmuddle, however, hardly pursued these speculations to their ultimate consequences, and his reflections went no farther than saying to himself:

"I remember reading somewhere of a veteran huntsman, who, when some one talked of the cruelty of fox-hunting, said, 'The men enjoy it, the horses enjoy it, the hounds enjoy it, and who knows that the fox may not enjoy it too?' Well, I think I can answer that question. If the fox feels at all as I did, when I had those confounded beasts close at my back, I am afraid it would be too great a stretch of the imagination to suppose that the fox enjoys it."

But then he reflected, that if there were no hunting there would be no foxes; so that, after all, it came to be a question whether the sum of vulpine happiness in living was a positive or negative quantity, as, if the former, it might be cheaply purchased at the cost of being hunted once or twice in the course of the season. And certainly if there was any truth in the economical axiom in favour of "the greatest happiness of the greatest number," there could not be a more signal instance of it than in a pursuit which gave pleasure to hundreds, at the expense of a doubtful balance of problematical evil to one predaceous little animal.

So when he recovered his wind and his horse, which had been caught and brought back to him, he mounted and rode after the hounds, and catching them up at their first check, went on with them for thirty minutes longer in an excellent run, and saw the fox run into in the open and broken up with all the honours, without any compunction or misgivings.

CHAPTER IX.

THE STEEPLE-CHASE.

TOWARDS the close of the season, Fitzmuddle had made such progress in the art of equitation, that Martingale began to think the time had come when he might realise the great object of his ambition—that of pulling off a good thing with Velocipede. There was a hunt cup contested annually over Tugby Steeple-chase Course, which always excited great interest, being confined to *bonâ fide* hunters who had been hunted regularly with the Thorn hounds and were ridden by their owners. Martingale felt very certain that Velocipede could beat any horse in the hunt, if his rider would follow his instructions and not tumble off, and he really thought that Fitzmuddle, with a little schooling, might manage to stick on. So he broached the subject to him. At first Fitz-muddle was staggered at the idea of riding a race, and felt very nervous at the notion of riding in a silk jacket over big fences in the presence of several thousand spectators. But Martingale encouraged him, and told him it was much easier to stick on over fences at a racing pace, than to take smaller obstacles in the hunting-field; and he took him up to Farmer Day's private course, and led him over some fences, which Fitzmuddle negotiated very successfully, so that at last he made up his mind to enter his horse.

When the name of "Mr. Fitzmuddle's chestnut horse, Velocipede, 11 stone 4 lb.," appeared in the entry for the "Hunt Cup, over two miles of the Tugby Course, owners to ride," there was much laughter at the club; and when Fitzmuddle, contrary to his usual wont, happened to look in that evening, he was assailed by a volley of chaff. "It was a shame of him not to give the other fellows a chance." "A rider like him ought to be handicapped with at least a stone more than the rest of the field." And so on;

but Captain Hardup took a more business-like view of the situation, and thought that perhaps Fitzmuddle's horse might be transmuted into a pony; or, in other words, that a pony might be made out of him. So he accosted Fitzmuddle: "Of course you want to back your horse. What do you say, will you take three ponies to one?" For the judicious Hardup knew well enough that the odds were certain to be not less than five to one, and, like Lord Augustus Fitzplantagenet in Byron's "Don Juan," he dearly loved to be

Good at all things, but better at a bet.

But Fitzmuddle replied: "No, I never bet. I have only just entered my horse for the fun of the thing, and to have some idea of what the sensation is like of flying over fences at a racing pace. And I am sure that, if by any miracle I did get first into the winning-field, some more accomplished jockey, like you, Hardup, or Lord Scamperton, would ride me out of the race, and do me on the post."

Now Hardup was keen for a bet, and he said:

"Oh, you think you will be first into the winning-field, do you? Make it £150 to £50, and I'll lay you that you are not." This rather riled Fitzmuddle, and on the spur of the moment he said "Done!" Then one of the young fellows, who thought himself a bit of a wag, said: "But we must have it quite clear. Which are you betting against, the man or the horse? Suppose Fitzmuddle tumbles off, and his horse goes on and comes in first, how about the bet?"

"Oh," said the captain, "in that case, of course I win, for, to tell the truth, it is the man rather than the horse I am betting against."

"Come, now," said the wag, "fair play's a jewel, and in that case if the man is first in the winning-field, you lose your bet." And the other fellows chimed in and declared that Fitzmuddle ought to have the off-chance of his horse refusing, and shooting him over his head at the last fence, and that the bet should be off if the captain would not agree. The captain was keen for the bet; so, after some demur, he assented, and the bet was duly booked thus:

"Captain Hardup bets Mr. Fitzmuddle £150 to £50 that Fitzmuddle is not first into the winning-field in the race for the Thorn Hunt Cup, provided that Mr. Fitzmuddle is to ride the course fairly up to the last fence, and not get off and jump that fence on foot."

When the eventful day drew near, Martingale came into his master's room and gave him sage advice.

"Gentlemen jockeys," he said, "who are new to the thing, if they happen to be mounted on the best horse, lose their races for want of a pace, and because they are afraid of making use of their mount. So they wait till the last field or two, and then get beaten for speed by some little scratchy thing that is quick on its legs, and has a good artist on its back who knows how to finish. Now this here Velocipede can stride along at a real racing pace, and though Lord Scamperton's and the Captain's have both a turn of speed when they are not blown, there is not one of them can live with our horse for a mile at a fair racing pace, and if you do blow him a little, why, you will blow the others ten times more, and the rest are of no account. So take my advice, and directly you are over the brook on the far side of the course, which is just a mile from home, you give the old horse his head and a touch of the spur, and come along. If you only do this, it is only a question of sticking on, and you can't lose the race."

Fitzmuddle pondered over this, and got up next morning at six, and went with Martingale up to the farm where the farmer had allowed him to take his gallops, and got on Logician, while Martingale mounted Velocipede and took him along for a mile just to give his master an idea of what he meant by a pace. And Fitzmuddle acquitted himself so well over the farmer's fences, that Martingale became quite hopeful and said to himself, "There is no five to one against in it, but rather five to one on our horse, for if master don't tumble off, and I don't think he will, we can't lose."

So the day came, and all the rank, beauty, and fashion of three counties were mustered on the stand, and in drags and carriages round the judge's chair, at Tugby Steeple-chase Course, and the neighbouring farmers and their wives and daughters were there, and a strong body of railway men and mechanics from Tugby Junction, and a sprinkling of gipsies and roughs, and a detachment of betting men had come down from London and made the air hideous with their hoarse shouts of 2 to 1 bar one.

After two other races the bell rang for the Thorn Hunt Cup, and seven competitors appeared.

Lord Scamperton's Diana .	*Rose.*
Captain Hardup's Blackleg .	*Black and White Cap.*
Mr. Fitzmuddle's Velocipede	*Green and Buff.*
Mr. Jones' Skyrocket . . .	*White, Blue Cap.*
Mr. Brown's Badger . . .	*Blue and White Stripe.*
Mr. Robinson's Rattler . .	*Chocolate, Yellow Sleeves.*
Mr. Smith's Scavenger . .	*Blue, Yellow Cap.*

The odds ranged: 6 to 4 against Diana, 2 to 1 Blackleg, 5 to 1 Velocipede, 7 to 1 Skyrocket, 10 to 1 any other.

The race was run almost exactly as Martingale predicted. Jones on Skyrocket made the running at no very great pace, but fast enough to dispose of half the field before they came to the brook. Brown's horse refused at the second fence, and was out of it; Robinson came a cropper over the third fence; and Smith was hopelessly tailed off before they had gone half-a-mile; Jones only kept his pride of place to the brook, and there Skyrocket being a little blown, stopped short, then shot up into the air like a rocket, shooting Jones up still higher, and both came down together with such a splash that the dirty water spoiled the smart gowns of three young ladies from Tugby, whom a gallant butcher had driven out in his cart, and stationed opposite to the brook in the hope of seeing some fun there.

This left Captain Hardup with a slight lead, with Lord Scamperton close on his right, and Fitzmuddle about a length behind on his left. They all flew the brook gallantly, Velocipede taking it in his stride so easily that his rider hardly felt him rise. Directly they were over the Captain put on a little more steam, being afraid that if he waited too long, Lord Scamperton's mare would beat him for speed. But Fitzmuddle, acting on Martingale's instructions, gave

Velocipede his head and a touch of the spur, and to the Captain's intense astonishment he shot past him in the twinkling of an eye, and took such a lead that the others had to sit down and ride in earnest to keep within hail of him. Field after field Velocipede kept striding along and gaining ground, though he lost a little at some of the fences to his more artistically-handled competitors. Still, he kept going like a steam-engine, and when they got into the last field but one he was leading by at least four lengths, and the hoarse roar of a thousand voices arose: "Velocipede wins, Velocipede walks in."

And, indeed, it looked very like it, for when he came to the last fence into the winning-field, which was a thick and high bushed-up hedge on a low bank, he had a lead of a good five lengths. But whether Fitzmuddle slightly overdid it, in driving his horse across that last field, which was of long grass, heavy and sloppy with rain, or whether in the excitement of finding himself so near home he forgot to sit still and hustled him at the fence, or whether the horse slipped in taking off or mis-judged the distance, will never be known; but the result was, that instead of clearing the hedge he crashed into it, and sent Fitzmuddle flying yards over his head into the winning-field. So there could be no doubt about his having won his bet, for the horse was five lengths before anything when he fell, and Fitzmuddle was a good two lengths before his horse.

The other two, though their horses were both beaten, managed to scramble over the hedge, and a punishing race ensued; but Diana had just the foot of Blackleg, and Lord Scamperton won by half a length.

Fitzmuddle, though badly shaken, was not much hurt, and managed to get up and walk to the stand. Hardup looked very glum, for he had lost a good deal on his own mount, as well as the bet to Fitzmuddle. At first he tried to dispute the latter, and act on the principle of " win, tie, or wrangle," but the case was too clear; for that Fitz-muddle had backed himself heavily, first into the win-ning-field, was undeniable, both from the mud on his

back, and the dent in the soft ground ; that he had
failed to negotiate a hedge was an obvious fact ; and
that he had carried off a big stake was apparent,
for there it lay where he had fallen, and a wide
rent in his leather breeches showed that nothing
but the proverbial fortune of the Fitzmuddles had
saved him from being impaled on it. So some
of the fellows in the hunt who had a grudge
against the Captain, because he had often fleeced
them at cards, swore that if he did not pay up like
a man, 'they would have him posted as a defaulter.
So Hardup had no help for it, and as he rode
home on the drag, he sat gnawing his moustache,
and revolving in his mind whether it would not be
better to make a bolt of it, and retire to the
breezes of Boulogne. But that night he dined
with Softy, the son of the rich banker, and the
champagne was good, and of the eight or ten
young fellows there, two or three drank freely
because they had won, and the rest more freely
because they had lost, while Hardup drank
discreetly, as he always did when there was a
prospect of cards after dinner. And sure enough

after dinner cards were produced, and Hardup proposed loo, and, to use his own phrase, forced the running by getting the stakes fixed pretty high. So the result was that he won £120 from Softy, £50 from Smith, and £20 from another fellow, who were all good for the money.

So he concluded that on the whole it would be better to postpone his trip to Boulogne, and go to Liverpool a man of honour and a gentleman, with £40 left after paying Fitzmuddle's bet, wherewith to back for the Grand National a horse, which from private information he thought was meant to be a real good thing.

So Fitzmuddle got his money, but when he went down to the stable, still feeling very stiff and sore, to. see how it fared with Velocipede, he found Martingale looking very disconsolate, for he had backed him for a tenner at five to one, and it is very mortifying when you thought £50 as good as in your pocket, to find it gone, and instead to have to hand over a couple of £5 notes. Fitzmuddle got out of him what was the matter, and told him of his own bet, which comforted

Martingale not a little to think that that sharper Hardup, as the stud grooms and gentleman's gentlemen were accustomed irreverently to call him, for he was no favourite with high or low, had been so hit by his master. But what comforted him still more was when Fitzmuddle said : " Really, Martingale, I cannot bear to think of your losing that bet, for it was my fault. You could not have missed your £50 if I had ridden better, and steadied the horse at the last fence. So as I have won £150 by a fluke, I shall feel far more happy if you will take £50 of it, and just repay me by looking well after the horses."

Some may think Fitzmuddle a fool for this piece of liberality, but in reality it turned out an excellent investment, for Martingale, who was a very decent fellow, and already fond of his master, from that day forth became such a devoted adherent, that he spent most of his time in picking up information about horses and scheming how to buy to the best advantage, and get the best price possible for the cast-offs. And as he was an excellent judge of a horse, and on good terms with all the leading dealers and stud grooms in the kingdom, and knew all the sporting farmers round about, he picked up wonderful bargains, so much so, that when some years afterwards Fitzmuddle happened to take an average of the price he had paid for his horses since he began hunting, he found that it only came to £130 per horse, though he had been better carried than many a man whose average had been over £200. So if he saved even £40 a horse on thirty or forty horses, he got a good return for that £50 which gladdened Martingale's heart, and converted him from an honest paid servant into a zealous and devoted friend.

So true is it that timely and judicious liberality is often the best economy.

CHAPTER X.

FITZMUDDLE'S SMASH.

FITZMUDDLE, though not much the worse for his fall, was a good deal shaken, and so stiff, that for the next week or ten days he could not mount a horse, which he regretted mainly because it was the closing week of the Thorn pack, and he would get no more hunting till next season. But as good luck would have it, the Duffershire pack in the next county were to have a bye-day the week after at the famous Wellington Gorse, from which they had that wonderful run many years ago, which he had often pored over with admiration in the pages of the *Sporting Magazine.* So, having now quite recovered from the effects of his fall, he sent over two of his horses to Foxborough, and went on there by rail the night before and slept at the "George."

In the morning he rode on to the meet, which was only three miles from Foxborough, and found a goodly array of the rank, fashion, and beauty of Duffershire assembled at the covert's side. But on this occasion the famous Gorse did not keep up its reputation, for they drew it blank.

They next drew Brampton Wood. This was a large covert, and much depended on getting a good start. The bulk of the field kept on the lower side, where foxes generally broke. But about a dozen, among whom were Fitzmuddle and two ladies, happened to be at the upper corner when a fine fox came out, and the hounds dashed after him with a hot scent. For about ten minutes these twelve had it all to themselves, but when they came within a field of the village of Stoke, the Scriptural saying was verified, as it often is in fox-hunting, "that the first shall be last and the last first;" for the fox, instead of holding on straight on the east side of the village, turned sharp to the right, skirted it, and then resumed his course for Corton Gorse. This let in the field, but quite threw out the leading dozen, who clattered down the road and through the village, making, like John Gilpin, the ducks and geese flutter, and the old women and children scuttle into safe corners. But the long winding street of the village curved in the wrong direction, and those who followed it had extremely little chance of seeing any more of the hounds, running as they did with a burning scent, heads up and sterns down, and so close together that a sheet would have covered them.

But just before they came to the village, the foremost lady, who was mounted on a clever little chestnut mare, turned off the road over a pretty stiff post and rail into the fields, calling out to Fitzmuddle, who happened to be next behind her :

" Come along, I know a way across the fields, and we will catch them long before they reach Corton Gorse."

Fitzmuddle followed, but the rest did not like the look of stiff new timber, though it was nothing out of the way for height, so they kept on through the village and lost the run. All, except one lady, the celebrated Mrs. Gay Spanker, who was famous for having knocked over more men and horses, and caused more spills, than any other man or woman in five shires. She was mounted on an equally well-known and dreaded black steed with a great white blaze down his face, and some irreverent wags christened the pair, "Death on the pale horse."

One peculiarity of this lady was, that the sight of anything resembling a lady's habit in front of her inspired her with frantic jealousy, so she whipped and spurred her pale-faced steed in the hope of overtaking and passing the leaders. For the first two fields all went well, for the fences were low, and the horses easily cleared them in their stride. But the third field presented a most uncompromising obstacle in the form of an extremely high and thick bullfinch, through which daylight could be seen at one place only. That was a sort of gap where the fence had been a good deal broken down, and for it the leading lady steered. But when she got near it, she saw it was at best but a very awkward place. The fence, it is true, was not very high, but it stood on a narrow bank, with barely room for a horse to drop a foot on the far side; then came a ditch of unknown width and depth, for it was so choked up with weeds and brambles that there was no seeing its beginning or end; and, worst of all, the ground broke away from the edge of the ditch into the next field, in a sharp incline of ten or twelve feet, so that if any one tried to negotiate the whole obstacle at a fly, nothing was more likely than that man and horse would come to grief.

So the lady pulled her mare up to a trot, and saying, " Now, Daisy dear, take care," put her at it. The intelligent animal seemed to understand what her mistress said, for she pricked her fine-pointed little ears, just popped over the fence, struck out with her hind feet against the bank, skimmed over the ditch, and when she lighted on the slope, had her hind legs under her so quickly that the hind feet almost touched the ground before the fore feet, and so she got safely over. She turned half round in her saddle and shouted to Fitzmuddle: "It's a nasty, trappy place; go steadily at it."

Fitzmuddle, with one lady before him and another behind, had no idea of shirking it, though it had been as high as a haystack and as wide and deep as the Grand Junction Canal, but he recognised the wisdom of this advice, and steadied his horse to a slow canter. But just as he had taken off and was in the air, Mrs. Gay Spanker rushed up like a whirlwind and gave him what may be appropriately called a lesson in "field billiards." For, by the same stroke, she both scored a brilliant canon and pocketed the red in the form of the unfortunate Fitzmuddle, who fell with his horse half in the ditch, half on the slope, and the two rolled promiscuously down it, sometimes one, sometimes the other uppermost. The horse struggled up and galloped on, but Fitzmuddle saw more stars in his eyes than he did on the memorable night when he walked up the glen with Maggie from the gillies' ball, and his wind was knocked out of him, and he felt a sharp pain in his right arm, and such an acute pain in his left ankle, that when he tried in a confused way to rise, he fairly fainted with the agony.

When he recovered his senses, he found himself in a position which, in his ordinary condition, would have terrified the natural modesty of his disposition, viz., in the arms of a young lady.

This is how it happened.

Mrs. Gay Spanker, with the momentum of her headlong career, cleared hedge, ditch, and almost landed at the bottom of the slope. Her horse floundered, and nearly came on his nose; but to do her justice, she was a good horsewoman, she stuck to the saddle, the horse recovered himself, and she galloped on. She never stopped to look back, for she was keen to catch her rival, and she had an uneasy consciousness that she had committed a gross breach of the unwritten law of the hunting-field by cutting in as she did, and that her wisest course was to get out of sight and escape detection. But the other lady turned round in her saddle before she had gone fifty yards to see how her followers had fared; and when she saw that Fitzmuddle lay still, and did not rise, and his horse galloped past her riderless, plastered over with mud, and wild with terror, she drew rein on the instant and rode back. Fitzmuddle lay motionless on his back with a face as white as a sheet.

"Good God!" she said, "the poor fellow is killed;" and jumped off in an instant. "Stand still, Daisy, like a good mare," she said; and the intelligent creature seemed to know every word she said, for giving herself a good shake she began to crop the grass. But the lady raised a clear young voice, not in a scream, but in a loud shout for help in case any one might be within hearing, and going down on her knees without minding the wet clay, looked anxiously into Fitzmuddle's face to see if she could discover any signs of life; and seeing that though his eyes were shut, the corners of his mouth twitched a little, and he seemed to utter something between low moaning and breathing, she sat down in a puddle, lifted his head gently on her lap, and looked round to see if there was any help coming.

She had not long to wait, for it came in the shape of a rustic in a smock-frock, who had caught Fitzmuddle's horse and was leading him back. Possibly some ray of that hope "which springs eternal in the human breast," had suggested to him that thus haply might he earn an odd shilling, and spend his evening after his work was over in the taproom parlour of the "Red Lion," with a jug of home-brewed beer. And possibly, oh! enrapturing thought, the owner of the horse might be rich and liberal, and the shilling might be half-a-crown, in which case he registered a silent vow in heaven that the pint of home-brewed should be a quart of the county brewer's very best and strongest XX.

But when he came up and saw the gentleman lying apparently dead, his look changed to one of consternation; his jaw fell, his wide mouth opened from ear to ear, and his goggle eyes seemed to dilate into the biggest gooseberries ever commemorated in a provincial newspaper. The lady knew him, for he was one of her father's parishioners.

"Hodge," she said, "don't stand grinning there, but look sharp, and do exactly what I tell you. First give me the hunting flask from that saddle, then get on the horse and ride as fast as you can to Farmer Pratt's—it's only two fields off through that gate. Tell him there's been an accident, and to send four men directly with a hurdle, and mind, some soft hay on it; and then tell Pratt or his son to take the horse and gallop off to Foxborough, and fetch Dr. Ross to the Rectory, and bid him to bring his splints and all his surgeon tools, for I fear there are bones broken; and tell one of the boys at the farm to run across to the Rectory and tell them there has been an accident, and I am bringing some one home on a hurdle, and they are to get the blue bedroom ready, and they need not send for the doctor for I have done it already, and he must be sure to tell them not to be alarmed, it's not me, but only a poor gentleman. Now, Hodge, are you sure you understand all this?"

"Yes, miss, I be quite sure."

"Well then, try and remember it, and if you carry the message all right there will be half-a-crown for you in the evening if you call at the Rectory."

Thus promptly did this energetic young lady think out the right thing to do, provide for every contingency and translate her thought into action.

To compare small things with great, it was as when the molecules of Von Moltke's brain, set vibrating by the news that MacMahon was marching to relieve Bazaine, started off a score of messages along the telegraph wires which we call nerves, which transmitted by other more material wires, in an hour's time changed the direction of the march of the Crown Prince's army of 200,000 men from west to north, and sent it thundering down on MacMahon's flank; while another army, detached from the force beleaguering Metz, headed him off on the east, and he and his army and Emperor were shut up in Sedan like rats in a trap, and the whole glittering and corrupt fabric of the Second Empire collapsed in a day, like the bursting of some rainbow-tinted bubble of stagnant water and mephitic gas, which disappears, leaving a foul odour behind.

But Hodge scrambled on the horse and went on his errand, and the lady, taking the flask, poured some of its contents down Fitzmuddle's throat. It was but very weak brandy and water, for he was one of the most temperate of men, but it revived him, and he opened his eyes, and found himself in the very compromising position we have indicated, with his head on a young lady's lap.

"Thank Heaven," she said; "he is not dead. But now tell me, where do you feel most hurt? How is your head?"

"I think my head is all right," gasped out Fitzmuddle; "though it seems to swim a bit. But my right arm feels rather bad, and I have a horrid pain in my left ankle."

"Ah! that's nothing," said the lady, who from her experience at the sick beds and sick clubs of the parish poor, had acquired some elementary notions of the science of surgery; "broken bones will heal. But now take a long breath, and tell me if you feel anything that seems to stab you inside."

He did so; but "No," he said, "nothing the matter there. But, good Heavens!" he said, "what am I thinking about? You are losing your run and sitting in the wet. I beg you ten thousand pardons; pray get up and go on. I will lie here right enough till some one comes." And the pale lips quivered with pain as he said it, and she thought to herself, "Well, whoever he is, he is a rare plucky fellow; and what is more, he is a gentleman. I wonder if he can be that Fitz-muddle they were all laughing at at Lady Sneerwell's the other night! There are precious few of those superfine swells who would ask me to ride on and not miss my run, if they had had a spill like that." But she spoke up and answered cheerily: "Ridiculous nonsense! Do you think I'm a brute to leave you here all alone with I don't know how many of your bones broken, and

all the fault of that horrid Mrs. Gay Spanker?
No, I mean to take you to the Rectory and have
you properly looked after, and your bones mended,
and you shall be in the saddle again soon, and we
will go out together next season, and cut down
old Death on the pale horse." From which it
may be gathered that Mrs. Spanker did not stand
very high in the young lady's good graces—which
is true, for she hated an unfair and jealous rider—
and it had come round to her ears that Mrs.
Spanker was constantly making spiteful remarks
about her riding and her looks, and the cut of her
habit.

But Fitzmuddle, with his face still twitching
with pain, and only swallowing down a groan by a
determined effort, said :

"But I should be awfully in the way. Pray
don't put yourselves out on my account. If I can
get carried to the inn I shall do very well there."

"Stuff!" she said, "your wits must be still
wool-gathering to think of such a thing. Inn,
indeed! I should rather think not. No, you cannot
help yourself, you are my captive, and must do as

I bid you ; and to the Rectory you go and remain there till you are able to move."

And whether Fitzmuddle was too exhausted to argue the point, or whether he thought that after all it might be nicer to be nursed by a pleasant young lady than by a dirty maid at a little country inn, it is certain that he made no more remonstrance.

But now the men arrived with the hurdle, and lifted Fitzmuddle carefully on it, and the lady made a pillow of the soft hay for his head, and they carried him to the Rectory like a wounded hero on his shield. And when they got there, the Rector, and his wife, and Jane the cook, and Alice the housemaid, and the gardener, all stood at the door, and there were exclamations of wonder and of pity, and then of pity and of wonder. But the young lady cut them all short, and had him carried upstairs to the blue bedroom and laid on the bed ; and, indeed, he was almost in a faint again, for, move him gently as they could, the pain was awful. So they gave him a half-glass of brandy, neat this time, and set to work to try and get off some of his clothes. And the Rector tried to cut them off with a large pair of scissors, but he was too nervous, and his hand shook; so the lady sent John the gardener to fetch a pair of pruning shears from the garden, and among them they managed to cut off his boots and coat, and slit up his leathers at the knee. And the women, if a bull may be permitted, stuck to their work manfully, and only stopped when things had come to the last extremity, that is, when they had got everything off except the last-mentioned habiliments and his flannel waist-coat. And they covered him over with the bed-clothes, except the ankle which could not bear even the pressure of a sheet, and that they kept bathing with a handkerchief dipped in eau-de-Cologne—it was one of the lady's best hand-kerchiefs, by the way, with a laced fringe; but perhaps Alice thought it might be the softest, or, in her hurry, she took the first that came to hand. And Jane suggested beef-tea and ran down to the kitchen to make it. And the Rector fidgeted about the room till his daughter told him he could

do no more good, and had better go downstairs
and wait till the doctor came. And she and
Alice sat down by the bedside, with that sweet
sympathy for physical suffering which is an
invariable attribute of the female heart, bathing
his ankle, and now and again bathing his brow,
and murmuring soft words of pity and consolation.

But the doctor soon came with his box of
implements and examined him all over, and pronounced that there was no internal injury, and
nothing but a compound fracture of the right arm,
and a very bad sprain, which almost amounted
to a dislocation, of the left ankle. So he bound
these up and put splints on, and got him made
quite comfortable, and administered a dose of
morphia, which lulled the pain and sent him off
into a sort of doze for the next twelve hours, and
left him, speaking cheery words that he would
have him up on the sofa in a week, and in the
saddle long before next season.

And here we must leave him and give some
account of our heroine and her belongings, for
that this prompt and decided young lady, who

picked him up and brought him home, is to be the heroine, is an open secret, which by this time the most obtuse of our male readers must have almost divined; while our fair readers, with that intuitive quickness of apprehension which characterises their sex in all matters appertaining to love and matrimony, have doubtless divined it long ago.

Miss Mary Morton was the only daughter of the Rev. John Morton, rector of the parish of Stoke-Regis in the county of Duffershire.

CHAPTER XI.

COURTSHIP.

THE Rev. Rector was a fine specimen of the good old Church of England parson, half saint and half squire, who attended to all his duties, visited the sick, relieved the poor, preached orthodox though slightly soporific sermons on Sundays, but on a week-day thought it no sin to attend occasionally the meets of the Duffershire hounds, in a black coat, and discuss the prospects of the crops, and the price of cattle, with the neighbouring landlords and farmers. He was liberal and charitable to an excess, spared no time or trouble in promoting schools, sick clubs, and all good works in his parish, and in fact, possessed all the virtues under the sun, except the cardinal one of making both ends meet, and finding himself at the end of the

year with a balance at his banker's. The younger
son of a good family, he was thought to be provided for by the family living, and left with a
small patrimony, which, as years went on, became
"small by degrees and beautifully less." He
married, while young, a penniless girl for love,
by whom he had two children, Frank, a fine,
gallant young fellow, who would go into the army,
and was now with his regiment in India; and our
heroine, Mary.

Mary Morton was what is called a real good
girl, honest as the day, frank and genial, but with
a rare gift of sterling common sense, and a latent
fund of energy and decision, which made her
invariably come to the front in all family difficulties; these qualities, implanted by Nature, had
been strengthened by the circumstances in which
she was placed. Her mother, Mrs. Morton, had
been for years an invalid, and the tender care
which her father lavished on the loved wife of
his youth, had been one cause of his pecuniary
troubles, for he thought nothing too good for her,
and spent hundreds in doctors' fees, and trips to

the sea-side and foreign watering-places. At the same time he anxiously kept these troubles from her, and shielded her from all domestic worries, lest they should disturb her shattered nerves.

Mrs. Morton, an amiable but not very strong-minded woman, acquiesced readily enough in this soothing treatment, and, although always kind and loving to her husband and children, quietly relapsed into a nonentity as far as all business affairs and household arrangements were concerned.

Frank was a good boy, and not at all extravagant, but a young man who goes into the army is not much at home, and costs money; and as long as his allowance of £200 a year, in addition to his pay, was paid punctually, he asked no questions, and concluded that everything was right at home.

Hence it came to pass, that as Mary grew up, Mr. Morton, who it must be confessed was not exactly a pillar of strength himself, came to lean more and more on her sounder sense and stronger nature. Thus, by degrees, she slid into the position of the undisputed head and manager, not only of the Morton household, but of the Morton finances and affairs generally. Perhaps it was this which gave at times an expression of manly strength and almost sternness to her pleasant and comely face, and drew down the corners of her full lips with a set look of decision. For Mary's face, in its usual sunshine, though not exactly that of a professional beauty, or made up of the catalogue of perfections usually ascribed to the heroines of novels, was a real pleasant face that did you good to look at. Clear, honest gray eyes that looked you straight in the face; a broad, white forehead, with plentiful clusters of dark-brown hair; a complexion that told of health and country air; and an expression that told as plainly of health of mind, sense, good nature, and a naturally happy disposition. What though her nose was not perhaps to a critical eye as finely chiselled, or her upper lip as short and curved as those of a Greek goddess; and the bloom on her cheek might be pronounced by some pallid votaress of London fashion to be that of a peach which the sun had wooed too ardently; the whole combination was a pleasant one in the eyes of Fitzmuddle, as I am sure it would be in the eyes of every male reader who can appreciate what is meant by a good, honest, modest, sensible English girl ; and, I would almost hope, by every female reader who was such herself, and whose taste had not been sophisticated by studying the fashionable monstrosities who squeeze their waists into the form of attenuated hour-glasses, and expand unmentionable regions into humps like those of dromedaries, while they smirk and simper at one another in the pages of the *Journal des Modes,* or the *Queen: the Lady's Newspaper.*

Such, at any rate, was not the figure of Mary Morton. She was such as Nature, and not a French milliner, made her: rather above the middle height, with a well-rounded though elastic figure, and a waist which may be aptly described as a *juste milieu,* or happy compromise, between that of a fashionable lady and our old friend Maggie Macdonald.

Such as she was, she was seated with her father in his library, on the black Boxing-Monday of the preceding Christmas, with a pile of accounts before them, and an open bank-book on the table, which showed a most attenuated balance.

"Papa dear," she said, "this will never do; this can never go on. Sims the butcher, and Brown the baker, are good men, but they can't go on supplying us with meat and bread for ever if we don't pay them at the end of each year; and there are the grocer, and the tailor, and the corn-factor, and the coal bill, and a host of others who ought all to be paid. It is not honest to take their goods if we cannot pay them. We are downright swindlers if we go on living at the rate of £1,200 a year when our income is barely £800."

"Too true, my dear," sighed the Rev. Morton, "but what can we do? Your mother's health requires constant attention; it would be hard on poor Frank to stop his allowance, and hard on me to give up all my subscriptions and charities; besides, how would all that help us in the present difficulty, how to tide over the next New Year? You see yourself it would take £800 at least to clear us, and we must have something to go on with till I get my next half-year's tithe."

" I have thought of all that," said Mary; "sell those shares in the Great Golconda Gold Mine, in which you would invest the last £2,000 we had left, though I would never have let you do it if I had but known."

For it must be known that one of the good Rector's weaknesses, and that which had contributed more than any other to his present impecuniosity, was a fatal facility for believing in gaudy prospectuses. Like most weak men he was a firm believer in his own luck, and no amount of failure could cure him of the fascination that he was destined some day to draw a great prize in the lottery of joint-stock companies, which would remove all his embarrassments, and enable him to indulge in the modest luxuries of taking his wife to Homburg, doubling Frank's allowance, and buying a first-rate hunter for his dear good Mary.

However, when brought suddenly to book by this matter-of-fact proposal, his brow darkened, and he said sadly: "It would be a thousand pities to part with the shares just as they have sent out the new crushing-machine, and are going to find gold enough to make us all rich. Moreover, between ourselves, they are not very marketable at present, and I don't think, if I forced a sale, I could get even £1,000 for them."

"I felt sure of that," said Mary, "so I have thought of another string to our bow. Mr. Barton, of the Duffershire Bank, is an old friend. Go to him, tell him your story, and ask him to give you a loan for a year of £1,000, on your own bond, with the security of those shares, and of a bill of sale over our furniture and effects, which are worth more than that. I am sure he will do it; then we will pay off all our debts and start clear with a balance of £200 at the bank, and you must give me *carte blanche* to cut our expenditure down to our income."

Mary's good sense and decision carried the day. The Rector rode with a heavy heart to the bank, and as Mary predicted, Mr. Barton, the senior partner, a kind-hearted though somewhat weak old man, though it was not a very proper banking transaction, gave the loan to oblige an old friend. Mary, with an equally heavy heart, sat down and wrote to Frank to tell him of the unavoidable necessity of stopping his allowance. Having got over this, which was the worst part of her task, she set to work bravely to encounter all the minor disagreeables incident to reducing an accustomed scale of expenditure. The butler was replaced by a neat parlour-maid, the coachman and head gardener were discharged, the carriage-horses sold, and a hard-working man, with a lad and a little occasional help, looked after the stable and the garden. She would have sold her own hunter at once, but was advised not to send her up to Tattersall's, where she would be thrown away, but to ride her occasionally to hounds through the rest of the season, and she would be sure to get £100 for her before it was over. Thus it was that she happened to be out with the hounds on the day when she acted the part of the good Samaritan to Fitzmuddle.

The cloud that hung over the Rectory was thus for a time dissipated, and Mary, whose brave, buoyant spirit, though always ready to face difficulties, never made herself wretched by anticipating them, was able to resume her usual duties, and at the same time to devote a good deal of attention to her interesting invalid, who, as the doctor predicted, had in a few days got down to a sofa in the library. She was a capital nurse, always ready and decided, but never fussy, and she and Fitzmuddle soon got to be excellent friends. She liked his simple, innocent ways, and felt a pleasure in doing him any little service, while he found her presence had a wonderfully soothing effect, and was never so happy as when she sat by the side of his sofa, and read to him, or talked to him so nicely and sensibly that he quite forgot to be shy, and after a few days felt quite at his ease. At last they got quite confidential, and as he was unable to use his right hand, Miss Morton was installed for the nonce as his private secretary, opened his letters and conducted his correspondence. Among others she wrote the following for Fitzmuddle to sign :

"MESSRS. COUTTS & CO.
" SIRS,

"Having broken my right arm, please note that I shall sign as under for the present with my left hand. Send me here my bank-book, as usual, made up to the end of the month.

"Yours faithfully,

" A. FITZMUDDLE."

Under this treatment he came out in quite a new light, and showed that so far from being a fool he really had a very fair understanding, and could take an interest in a great many things that neither he nor any one else had given him credit for.

"Do you like poetry?" asked Miss Morton one wet afternoon. "Shall I read you a bit of my favourite Tennyson?"

"I am afraid, Miss Morton," he said, "that the gods have not made me poetical. I tried

Swinburne once, and Browning, but really I could not make head or tail of them. However, anything you like I am sure I shall like, so please read away and I will listen."

She took the " Idylls of the King," and in a low, musical voice, quite natural though full of feeling, read him the tale of Launcelot and Elaine.

He got quite excited over it, and said : " Why, what a fool he was not to marry that dear, sweet girl, Elaine, and what brutes he and Guinevere must have been to behave as they did to good King Arthur!"

She was amused at his indignation, and said : " But you see they were not quite so bad, for Launcelot had got from the Lady of the Lake at his birth a fatal gift of fascination, which made all the ladies fall in love with him. So it was a sort of fate, like what we read of in the Greek tragedies ; and I sometimes think that Tennyson must have meant, under the guise of this fable, to give us the tragedy which is just as true now as then, of noble souls drawn by some resistless destiny into false positions, where they sin and suffer without altogether losing their nobility of nature."

"By Jove!" he said, "what a clever girl you are; you read books and see in them things I should never have seen, and yet when you explain them they seem quite obvious."

And so they read more Tennyson together, and the story of Enid specially took his fancy, and he began to build castles in the air, and dream how, if he were only a noble knight like Geraint, he would kiss the fair hand that brought him his tea and toast and morning newspaper, and do some heroic action which should entitle him to claim it as his own.

Thus he slid day by day farther down the flowery slope, until he was much too far down to think of recovery, and, to use the common phrase, was "over head and ears in love."

But she stood hovering on the brink, for she was too good and sensible a girl to fall in love without some assurance that her love would be returned; and with all her strength of character she had, at bottom, a fund of diffidence in herself and her own attractions, which made her slow to believe that a little pleasant intercourse and harmless admiration from a man shut up in a dull country parsonage, really meant anything so serious as committing matrimony with a penniless girl with a wide mouth, and a nose slightly *retroussé*.

Perhaps her experiences of the male sex had been adverse to much belief in the capacity of young men of the present day to marry for love. Like most young women who have reached the mature age of twenty-two, she had "dreamed her dreams," and fancied once or twice that the true prince had come. The first was a dashing young cavalry officer whom Frank brought down with him during their long leave for a month's hunting. But he, like many another bold dragoon, "made love and rode away." Then came Mr. Chasuble, her father's curate, who read poetry with her, poured sentimental nonsense into her ear under the disguise of spiritual experiences, and generally led her to believe that he was in a state of ecstatic despair if she frowned, and of seraphic delight if she smiled. But somehow his tale of love sounded a little too unctuous and ecclesiastical to be quite to her mind, and it was with a feeling of relief rather than of disappointment that she heard, that having gone to Scarborough to recruit his health, shattered by the violence of his emotions, he had become engaged there to a soap-boiler's widow, ten years older than himself, but with the solid attraction of a fortune of £20,000 at her own disposal.

Thus Mary Morton had escaped without any serious wound from the illusions of her youthful imagination, but had been just near enough the fire to make her feel, like the burnt child, that it was safer to keep away from it, and to make her require some strong outward impulse to break through the barriers of her reserve.

This impulse soon came in an unexpected way. The cloud, which had been dispelled for a time by the arrangement with the bank, burst one morning suddenly like thunder from a summer sky.

On taking up the county newspaper at breakfast, the following announcement, in the largest type, caught the astounded eye of the worthy Rector:

"FAILURE OF THE DUFFERSHIRE BANK.

"We regret to say that this old and highly respectable institution has suspended payment. It is due to the senior partner, Mr. Barton, to state that he is in no way responsible for this lamentable event, which took him completely by surprise; but it appears that the junior partner, Mr. Dicey, who has latterly taken the chief part in the management, owing to Mr. Barton's advancing years and declining health, had become involved in large speculations on the London Stock Exchange, to support which he had used the credit and reserves of the Bank to an alarming extent. We fear this stoppage will cause great inconvenience throughout the district, as so many of the county gentry and farmers kept their accounts there, and, of course, will be unable to draw out the balances on which they had reckoned to meet current expenses; while those, and we fear there are many, who have had advances from the bank will be compelled to discharge them at once, as the bank will be thrown into liquidation."

No wonder the Rector dropped the untasted toast from his mouth, and fell back in his chair with a heavy groan.

"What on earth is it, papa?" cried Mary; "nothing bad about Frank, I hope!" and she snatched the paper from his hand with a sudden feeling of tightness about the heart, and read the ominous paragraph. "Thank God!" she said, "it is not Frank, only the bank."

"Only the bank!" said the Rector; "why, surely that is bad enough—what on earth is to become of us?"

Mary paused a moment, and her head seemed to swim, but she rallied in an instant, and felt that if she gave way all was lost.

"After all, papa," she said, "it might be worse, we have paid off all our little debts; perhaps it is not so bad as it looks, and we may have time to turn round, and, if the worst comes to the worst, we can sell all the things here, which will pay the bank, and go into lodgings, and I will be your maid-of-all-work. Depend upon it, things seldom turn out quite so bad or quite so good, as we feared or hoped at the first blush."

So the brave girl met the blow, and did her best to cheer and comfort her parents. But brave as she was, she received another blow which, for the time, quite broke her down, and made her feel that Fate is stronger than the strongest will.

Next morning among the letters was one addressed to her, with an Indian post-mark, and in the well-known handwriting of her brother Frank. She snatched it up and retired to the library to read it. It ran thus:

"MY OWN DEAR SISTER,

"I am in desperate trouble, and as usual fly to you, as I know you will help me if you can, and if any one can it is you. I got your letter as to poor father's affairs, and how you had been obliged to stop my allowance. You did quite right, and it was no one's fault, and, as you say, it would have been swindling to go on running up bills we knew we could not pay. So I don't say a word of complaint, but it came at a most unlucky time for me. I have been put to a lot of expenses lately, which I really could not help. There was the move of the regiment, no end of subscriptions for bands, balls, etc., in which I was obliged to share; I had to advance money to poor Nesbitt of ours, to give him a chance of living by going home—in vain, for he died, poor fellow, on board the steamer, but it took a lot of my ready. And then, to crown all, my horse died, and I had to buy another, and, like a fool, I bought a gray horse from a fellow in the 19th, which I knew had the foot of all in our regiment, and like a still greater fool (this is for your own private ear, dear Mary), put £50 on him at 4 to 1 for our races, hoping to get back the money I wanted. And so I should, but as ill-luck would have it, he broke down when winning in a canter.

"So that is about where I was when I got your letter: my mess bills not paid, £100 owing for

the horse, and £50 for the bet, and both to
fellows who would not give me a month's time
to save my life. What on earth was I to do?
As a last resource I went to Binnie of the Agra
Bank, who is a great pal of mine, and a real good
fellow, and asked him to cash a bill for me on
Cox's for £200. Binnie looked grave and said:
'My dear fellow, I would do it for you with
pleasure, but I hope you know what you are
about, and are quite sure the money will be at
Cox's to meet it. You know what happened
when those two men in the 1st Diddlesex paid
their debts in India by bills not worth the paper
they were written on, how they had to leave
the army, and the Commander-in-Chief got into
a furious rage, and swore he would have no
swindlers in Her Majesty's service, and would
cashier the first officer who drew a bill without
the means of meeting it, if he was his own brother.
And you know Sir Hector is a man of his word,
so be careful, and don't ask me to cash this bill
unless you are sure it will be met.'

"Well, this made me wince, but 'needs must when the devil drives,' and I felt sure that however badly my father might be off for money, he would not like to see all my prospects blasted and have me turned out of the army with disgrace for £200. And, dearest Mary, I felt the greatest confidence in your clear business head seeing some way to pull me through. If you can't, I am very sure it is not for want of will but from sheer impossibility, and I must just grin and bear it, and, I suppose, dive under and go to the diggings. But if you can but manage to have £200 paid to my credit at Cox's by the 1st May, when the bill will be presented, it will be all right. You know me too well to think I would ever ask or take another farthing, while my father and mother are obliged to deny themselves their ordinary comforts ; and between ourselves, I have some good friends here on the Viceroy's staff, and if I can weather this storm, am almost certain to get a good staff appointment soon, which would enable me to help them instead of their helping me.

"So now, dearest Mary, you know the whole story, and I am sure you will do, as you always do, what is best and wisest.

"Your affectionate,

"but not over happy brother,

"FRANK MORTON."

The letter dropped from her hands. The 1st of May, and this was the 28th of April, and only £10 in the house, and no deposit to draw on at the bank. Oh! if she had only got the letter a week ago, when a cheque on the bank would have been honoured! No wonder she had that thrill at the heart about Frank, when the news came of the failure! And poor Frank, the bright, good boy, her only brother, who had been such a pride and pleasure to them all!

For the first time in her life she felt fairly overwhelmed, and sank back in her chair with a burst of tears. Just then the door opened, and Fitzmuddle, who could now hobble about with a stick, came into the room where his sofa was drawn near the window, and he was accustomed to lie all day, and talk to Mary or think about her.

It was too late to hide her tears. Fitzmuddle saw them at a glance, and with intense agitation stammered out:

"Dear me, Miss Morton, what on earth is the matter? I beg your pardon, but I am sure it is something dreadful to make you cry. I can't bear to see it, indeed I can't; I don't want to intrude, but pray tell me if there is anything I can do for you. Or, perhaps, you would rather I left the room."

"No, Mr. Fitzmuddle," she said, "it is only some family troubles which we don't want to bother a visitor with. Don't stand—lie down on the sofa, and I will go upstairs and have my cry out and think matters over, and then wash my face and come down."

With that she rose hastily and rushed out of the room, putting the unhappy letter, as she supposed, into her pocket, but in her agitation she missed the pocket and put it in a fold of her dress, and it fell on the floor. When she shut the door, Fitzmuddle saw the letter lying there and picked it up. He held it in his hand and looked anxiously at it. " I am sure," he said, "that is the letter which made her cry. I wish I knew what is in it, for perhaps I might be able to do something to help." And then he looked again, and wondered if he might not venture to have a peep at it. But then he reflected that young ladies' troubles were generally supposed to be connected with love, and that this was very likely a letter from some fellow in India (for he saw the post-mark) to whom she was engaged.

If so, it would be mean to read it, and Miss Morton would never forgive him if she knew it. And so he was about to replace the letter in her desk, when his eye almost involuntarily caught the signature of " Frank Morton."

" Frank Morton," he said, " why, that's her brother; there can't be any great harm in reading what her brother writes her, and ten to one it is some money trouble in which I could help." So he read it through, and looking very grave, carefully replaced it in the blotting-book inside the writing-desk, and hobbled back to his own room.

What he did there will presently appear.

In the meantime, Mary had her cry out in her own room, and began to think the matter over. Her brow knit, and her lips were drawn down, till at last she thought of the only thing possible to do, when her lips relaxed, she got up, washed away the trace of tears, and wishing to read the letter again before putting her plan into execution, put her hand into her pocket for it. To her dismay it was not there, but she thought possibly she had left it in the blotting-case, and only fancied in her hurry that she had put it into her pocket. So she ran downstairs, found the room empty and the desk shut, and the blotting-case in it just as she left them. She opened the case, and there lay the letter folded up with the last page and Frank's signature alone visible. " Ah," she said, " it is all right, no one can have possibly seen it, and I must have made a mistake about putting it into my pocket. No wonder, for my wits were wool-gathering."

She read it carefully over again, and then sat down and wrote the following letter:

"MESSRS. COX & CO.
" SIRS,

"A letter from my brother, Lieutenant Morton, of the Duffershire Light Infantry, now in India, informs me that a bill of his for £200 will be presented to you for payment by the Agra Bank on the 1st of May. It is of vital importance to him that this bill should be honoured, and when he drew it he had every reason to feel certain that the money would be lodged with you before that day. But owing to the failure of the Duffershire Bank, of which you have doubtless heard, it has become impossible for his father, the Rev. Mr. Morton, of Stoke Rectory, to find even this moderate sum at such a short notice. In this emergency, I can think of only one plan to save my brother from ruin. I have an annuity of £25 a year, left me by an aunt who died two years ago. It would be an act of real charity if you would sell this annuity for me, which, as I am only twenty-two years of age and in good health, should be worth more than £200, and in the meantime advance the money to meet the bill. I will give you my promissory note, and execute any assignment of the annuity you think necessary, and if you send me a telegram I will run up to London by the next train to sign any deed. In the meantime, I can only appeal to your generosity to comply with this urgent request if it is at all possible.

"I remain,

"Yours faithfully,

"MARY MORTON."

Next day, the evening post brought a letter from London to Miss Morton. Her heart beat so that she could hardly open it, but on doing so, what was her surprise and delight to find that it ran as follows :

"MADAM,

"Your favour of yesterday was duly received. It is quite unnecessary for us to avail ourselves of your generous offer, as a cheque for £200 was this morning paid to the credit of Lieutenant Morton's account here, by a friend whose name we are under strict injunctions not to mention.

> "We remain,
>> "Your obedient Servants,
>>> "Cox & Co."

She fell back in her chair, with a sigh of relief, and pressed her hands tightly on her eyes to keep in the tears—this time joyful tears—which welled up in them; and then with a start withdrew them, to satisfy herself by reading the letter again, that it was not an illusion, and that she was awake in the library, and not in bed dreaming. But, no: it was all right—the letter was there, brief and business-like, and there could be no doubt whatever about it; her dear brother, her darling Frank, was saved!

"Who could it be; who on earth could it be?" she asked herself, and her prophetic soul by a sort of instinctive divination reverted to Fitzmuddle.

"It is just the sort of thing he would do," she said, "he is so good and generous." But then she thought, "How could he possibly have known? I never said a word, and he could not have seen the letter, for there it lay inside the blotting-case inside my desk, just as I left it." More probably Frank had told his trouble to one of those good friends in India whom he wrote about, who had written or telegraphed home and lodged the money.

But still a sort of instinct in her heart kept repeating Fitzmuddle. Could she but know—could she venture to ask him? But, no. If, as her common sense told her, it was more probably some one else, how indelicate it would seem to hint that she had half expected and half hoped that he had sent the cheque! No, she could not ask Fitzmuddle such a question, and must wait for time to solve the mystery. In the meantime there was one thing she must do, and that was, not to keep poor Frank in suspense a minute longer than was necessary; so she wrote out a telegram to him, " All right, bill paid," and took it down her-

self to the post-office, and despatched it to India.
She then took a long walk across the fields to
collect her spirits and soothe her agitated nerves.
But all the time she kept saying to herself, "Whoever could it be?" and sometimes the needle of
her thoughts pointed to the unknown Indian
friend, and sometimes it swung round and pointed
Fitzmuddle-wards.

However, she had not to wait long for the
solution of the mystery, which came about, I am
sorry to say, not by the apparition of any ghost or
lady in white, or other expedient dear to the
soul of readers of sensational novels, but in the
following plain, prosaic, and matter-of-fact manner.

For the next two days she had felt quite shy
and embarrassed when alone with Fitzmuddle, and
the poor fellow felt quite miserable, thinking he
had offended her. But on the third day, when she
came into the library to bring him in his cup of
afternoon tea, he mustered courage to say :

"I hope you are not angry ·with me, Miss
Morton. I really could not help finding you so
upset the other morning. I would never have

thought of coming into the room if I had known I was intruding."

"Dear me, no," replied Miss Morton. "I angry with you? How could you possibly think such a thing? I was only upset about some family matters which are all right now, and it is I who ought to ask your pardon, if I have neglected my patient for the last two days."

Fitzmuddle brightened up immediately, and said : "Well, if you are not angry, show me that we are as good friends as ever by sitting down for a few minutes if you have no particular engagement, and helping me, as you used to do in the good old time, with this batch of letters. You see a fellow with a broken arm is no great hand at writing letters; and, by-the-bye, would you mind just looking over this bank-book, and seeing if you can find out a mistake? They send me my book at the end of every month, and somehow they make the balance a good deal short of what I make it out by my own note of my cheques."

She opened the bank-book, and the last entry in it at once caught her eye :

"*April* 30*th.*—Morton, £200."

She threw down the book, fell on her knees beside the sofa, caught Fitzmuddle's uninjured hand, and gave it a fervent kiss, exclaiming in broken accents:

"Ah, you are our saviour.   Something told me it from the first, and now I have found it out; it was you who sent that cheque to Cox, which saved poor Frank from ruin and disgrace.   May Heaven ever bless you!"

Fitzmuddle blushed up to the roots of his hair, and began to stammer out apologies. "Pray don't, Miss Morton; pray get up, and don't talk like that.   I know it was a great liberty to take, but I never thought you would have found me out; nor would you if I had not stupidly forgotten to enter that £200 cheque, and so got into a muddle about my balance.   But I really did not mean to intrude on your private affairs, and hope you will excuse me."

"Excuse you, indeed!" said Miss Morton. "Excuse you for what? For doing the most noble, generous action that ever was done on this earth, and saving my brother from utter ruin, and my father and mother from dying of broken hearts? But tell me, how did you ever come to know anything about it?"

Fitzmuddle blushed more furiously than ever, and said: "I am almost ashamed to confess, but it's no good telling a lie, and you are so clever you would be sure to find me out. I did a very mean, dishonourable thing, and read your letter."

"But how could that be?" said Mary. "I found the letter just where I put it, inside my blotting-case."

"For once you are wrong, Miss Morton," said Fitzmuddle, "*you* did not put it there, but *I* did; you dropped it on the floor, and I picked it up and read it, but pray believe me, I would never have done such a thing if my eye had not caught the signature, 'Frank Morton,' just as I was in the act of putting it back; and then I thought, 'Oh, if it is her brother there can be no great harm in a fellow reading it, and ten to one the trouble is about money, and I may be able to help.' For to tell the truth, Miss Morton, I could not bear to see you crying, and it put me in such a flutter that I hardly knew what I was about, so I hope you will not be very angry with me, though I own I read your letter."

Miss Morton's heart rose to her throat, and she said in a choking voice : " Why, you are heaping coals of fire on my head ; you do the most noble, generous act, and then you try to conceal it, and make me as many apologies as if you had ruined instead of saving us. How can I ever repay you ? "

A sudden inspiration seized Fitzmuddle, a sudden flush of courage rose to his face, and he said :

" There is one way in which you could repay me a hundred times over, and that is if you would give me the right to draw your cheques and read your letters for the rest of my life. Oh, Miss Morton, if you would only take pity on a poor fellow, and condescend to be my wife, I would be the happiest man in existence ; and I really think with a wife like you I might be made something of."

Miss Morton grew grave in an instant and said :

"Mr. Fitzmuddle, you do me the greatest possible honour, and my doubt is not whether you are good enough for me, but whether I am good enough for you. But this takes me quite by surprise. I had no idea of anything of the sort, and I must not repay you for your generous kindness by allowing you to engage yourself, unless I feel quite sure that I can love you as you deserve to be loved, and can be to you all that a good and true wife ought to be. You must give me till to-morrow morning to think it over and decide. It is a habit I have got into to think anything important well over by myself, before I finally decide."

And with that, in spite of Fitzmuddle's pro-testations that she was far too good for him, and that he was quite willing to chance it, she rose and left the room, making an appointment to meet him there next morning and give him her answer, so as not to keep him in suspense.

Poor Fitzmuddle was left in a state of great

inward trepidation. He could not bring himself to believe that such a grand, glorious girl could really care for a fellow like him, who had been brought up like a muff, and was always getting into some absurd scrape that made him look like a fool. "No," he said, "if she won't have me, I shall certainly go to the bad if I remain in England, and end by becoming a fool or worse, as well as looking like one. I'll be off to South Africa, and there I am certain to stumble into the mouth of some lion, or get in the way of a rhinoceros, and there will be an end of me; and better, too, than if I were to hang on about the West End of London, and Newmarket, and Melton, betting, gambling, drinking, and running after loose women, just to try to still the pain in my heart that was aching for Mary Morton."

Mary, on the other hand, gave what was for her the unusual excuse of a headache, to go to bed early, but not to sleep, for she lay awake half the night, resolutely thinking the matter over, and trying to come to a right decision. She was not enough in love to let her feelings run away with her reason; but was she in love enough, or did she feel that she could become so, to make an honest, true wife, and to feel certain that she was not marrying him for his money and position, or in a passing fit of gratitude for what he had done for her brother? Was she quite sure that she loved him well enough not to feel ashamed when others laughed at him? And did she think she could be a worthy help-mate to him, and make him be seen by the world the noble, generous, simple-minded gentleman which she knew him to be? She pondered on these things till far in the night, and, being unable to sleep, she rose and opened the window and looked out at the stars, and the still, solemn night brought gentle influences and sweet counsels. She seemed to see the poor pale face lying on her lap, and the white, quivering lips parted to beg her not to lose her run, and let him lie. She thought how pleasant it had been to trot backwards and forwards to the library with his cup of tea and newspaper, and to sit reading to him, and see his intelligence bursting out like a spring flower

T 2

after a winter's frost. She thought how dull the
Rectory would be if he went away, and wondered if
she should ever return to the old life, with its little
daily round of little duties, and fill up week after
week, and year after year, with visits to the
poor, teaching Sunday classes, and trying to bring
cosmos out of chaos with tradesmen's bills and
domestic expenses.

And then she thought of that crowning act,
the cheque for £200, and if possible, even more
of the generous nature that strove so hard to
conceal it, and instead of using it as a means of
pressing his suit, unfeignedly thought it a thing
to be apologised for. "I have had to be the man
of the family so long," she said, "that I almost
feared I had got a man's heart and lost my
woman's nature. But now I know that I have a
woman's heart still, and can be soft and love if
I am loved in return ; and what sort of a heart
should I have if it were not touched by such
noble, knightly devotion, and how can I repay
it better, or work out a more useful and happy
career for myself for the rest of my life, than

by devoting myself to him and trying to make him as happy and respected as he deserves to be? So now my mind is made up, and I will go to sleep."

And sleep she did soundly and with happy dreams, till half-past seven o'clock, when Alice called her. She rose and dressed slowly with the rays of the morning sun streaming in through the fresh green and blushing roses that twined about her window, thinking how he would look and what he would say.

"I will wager anything," she said, "he is fancying at this very moment that I am going to say 'No,' he is so very modest; well, that is a fault on the right side, for there is mighty little modesty going among the young men of the present generation as far as I have seen."

And truly enough, Fitzmuddle, who had been already in the library for half-an-hour, to the astonishment of the housemaid, who had just begun to sweep it out, had worked himself up to the conviction that it was utterly impossible that Miss Morton could accept him. "If she meant 'Yes,'" he said to himself, "she would have said 'Yes,' yesterday. But she meant 'No,' though her kind heart would not let her pain me by saying it right off, just after she had found out about the cheque for her brother. Well, well, if it is as I fear, I suppose I must make up my mind to grin and bear it."

The door opened and Mary entered. Any cool and dispassionate observer might have seen that her face, though grave, looked happy. But Fitzmuddle, who was neither cool nor dispassionate, saw only the gravity and not the happiness.

"Tell me my fate, Miss Morton, don't keep me in suspense, though I am afraid I know it already. It can be nothing but 'No' to such a poor fellow as I am."

"For once you are wrong," said Mary. "I have thought it over and slept on it, and it's not 'No,' but 'Yes.' So if you are in the same mind as you were yesterday, and really want to marry a poor penniless parson's daughter, I am yours for life, and I am quite sure I love you and will do my best to make you a true, good wife."

Fitzmuddle's transports of bewildered delight may be more easily imagined than told. In fact, the few first minutes of a scene like this are apt to be somewhat incoherent, and take the form of the broken ejaculations and emphatic gesture-language of our Palæolithic ancestors, rather than that of the spoken speech of civilised societies. Novelists would on the whole do best to leave these first rapturous five minutes to the imagination, and take up the thread of their narrative again when reason begins to return, and connected sentences are less broken up by osculatory interruptions.

The first sign of this returning rationality was afforded by Fitzmuddle's whispering in Mary's ear:

"But tell me truly, darling, how did you ever manage to fall the least little bit in love with a fellow like me, who is not the least of a lady's man?"

"Well, Augustus dear," she replied, "the first time I heard your name mentioned was at a hunting dinner, where a lot of supercilious young swells were laughing at you. I knew what a set of empty-headed idiots they were, so it set me against them, and I said to myself, 'I should not wonder after all if this Fitzmuddle is a better fellow than any of those asses, who have no idea of judging of a man by any other standard than the cut of his coat and the colour of his boots, and whose intellectual resources are confined to slangy talk about dogs and horses, and coarse talk about women.' Well, my first introduction to you was a day or two afterwards, when that horrid Mrs. Gay Spanker knocked you over and broke your bones, and I never could quite forget how your poor head lay in my lap, and your pluck in bearing the pain, and your courtesy in bidding me go on and not lose my run. I don't think Sir Launcelot himself could have shown such true courtesy. And then you were brought home and I nursed you, and you know from Elaine's fate that nursing wounded knights is a dangerous occupation, though my Launcelot is not going to ride away and leave poor me to die of a broken heart, and float down the river in a black barge. And then, and then—what finished the business, and quite did for me, was that charming love-letter you wrote."

"I wrote you a love-letter? On my honour I never thought of doing such a thing. What on earth are you talking about? I had quite enough to do to screw my courage up to speaking, let alone writing, which I never was much of a hand at."

"Yes, you did, sir," said Mary, with an arch smile; "you wrote the most eloquent love-letter, to my mind, that was ever penned. Pray who wrote 'Pay Lieutenant Morton or bearer £200'? That's what a letter ought to be, to my mind: short and sweet, and coming straight to the point. It was worth a whole reamful of darts and Cupids, and the usual rubbish of that sort, fit only to raise a laugh in an action for breach of promise."

"Well, I declare," said Fitzmuddle, "I am just the luckiest fellow in the world. Whenever I get into a mess it turns out to be the best thing that could have happened. If Mrs. Spanker had ridden fair, I should not have been knocked over and broken my bones; if I had not broken my bones you would not have picked me up and taken me to the Rectory; if that bank had not failed, and Frank got into that scrape just at the right time, you would never have needed the cheque; if I had not been mean enough to read your letter I should have known nothing about it; if I could have used my right hand and had not got into a muddle about my balance, you would never have found it out. And now the end is, that you are the dearest, best girl in the world, and I the happiest fellow."

"Well, Augustus dear," laughed Mary, "it really hangs together like the tale of the house that Jack built. And do you really and truly not repent, and mean to marry the 'maiden all forlorn'?"

The answer was given in that inarticulate primitive language to which we have alluded, though when lips come together, soul often says to soul a great deal more than could be conveyed by the choicest spoken language.

"But now," said Mary, "I must go and tell

papa and mamma, and not keep them waiting
for breakfast any longer."

Fitzmuddle's face became anxious.

"You don't think they will object, do you?"

"Well," said Mary, "I think I have conducted
more difficult negotiations to a successful issue;
so do you trust to me, and lie there, like a good
boy, and rest your poor ankle till I come back.
I won't be many minutes gone."

The Rector and his wife had been wondering
why Mary, who was usually so punctual, did not
appear.

"Perhaps she has got a headache still, poor
thing, and won't come down to breakfast," said
Mrs. Morton. "Do step up, dear, and knock at
her door, and see if there is anything the matter."

Mary entered with a beaming face, which told
that last night's headache was, at any rate, not
the cause of her unusual delay. She kissed them
both, and said:

"I have got a bit of news for you this
morning, you good old dears. I will give you
a penny if you can guess it."

"Nothing bad," said the Rector. "I can see that by your face. Is it the Golconda Mine? Have they struck gold?"

"Better than ten thousand Golcondas," said Mary; "read that," and she held out Frank's letter.

"Good God!" said the Rector, when he came to the end; "do you call that good news? Why, the girl is mad. Poor, poor Frank, it will break our hearts if this be true!"

"It's all right, you dear old goose," said Mary. "The money's paid, and the man who paid it never said a word about it, till I found him out, and now he has asked me to marry him, and I have said yes, and you ought to thank Heaven for sending your daughter such a husband, and you such a son-in-law."

And then there were transports of astonishment and delight, and Mary had to tell the whole story, and her mother kept repeating: "But is it really true? Are you quite sure there is no mistake?" and the Rector had to take his spectacles off and wipe them, for somehow they had got so dim that he could hardly see his Mary's face, and he kept on exclaiming :

"What a noble fellow! Who would have thought it possible? How can we ever thank him?"

"Come into the library," said Mary, "and thank him yourselves, for he is waiting there in sad alarm lest you two tyrannical parents should interpose obstacles."

So they went into the library and tried to thank him, but their voices broke down, and the good old Rector could get nothing out but :

"May God reward you. I can give you nothing for what you have done but an old man's blessing."

"Oh, I say!" said Fitzmuddle, "you must not take it like that. You can repay me ten times over if you will give me my own dear Mary, and let me try to be a second son to you, the same as your own boy in India."

So the tears were dried up, and when, after ten minutes spent in congratulations and explanations, they adjourned to the breakfast-room, though the breakfast was cold and the tea bitter, I doubt if a happier quartet ever sat down to a morning meal.

But there was great commotion downstairs at these extraordinary proceedings. What could possibly be the meaning of this delay in breakfast, and of these mysterious comings and goings between the morning-room and the library?

"I tell you what it is," said Jane the cook, who was of a romantic turn of mind, to Alice the housemaid; "what did I say to you the other night when we were reading that delightful story of the 'Wounded Baron and the Fair Chatelaine'? Did not I say, why, it's just like what is going on in this house this very blessed day? There is Mr. Fitzmuddle carried to the Rectory, just as the Baron was to the Castle, and he can't choose but fall in love with our Miss Mary, so good and sweet as she is, and mark my words, the end of it will be a marriage at our parish church, with silks and satins, and orange-blossoms, and bridesmaids, and everything that is delightful."

"Sure enough you said so," said Alice, "but I

wonder if it can really be true. Do you think we could ask her? Suppose you do, you have been longest in the house."

"Yes," said Jane, "but I have been mostly in the kitchen, and you have been most with her. Do you speak up and ask her; she won't be angry."

However, at last they agreed to go together for mutual support, so they went upstairs to her bedroom, and knocked at the door.

"Come in," said Mary; "what do you want, girls?"

Alice was the spokesman, but she felt fluttered and excited, and blushed and broke down, after "If you please, miss."

"Out with it," said Mary. "I won't eat you up, whatever it is."

"Please, miss," said Alice, "Jane and I have got it into our heads that we might have something to congratulate you about, and if it is so, we should like to be the first to wish you joy."

"Alice, and you, Jane," said Mary, "you have been good girls, and stuck to us in our troubles, and never grumbled at the extra work, so I look on you both as friends rather than servants; and it won't be long secret, and every one will know it in a day or two, so I don't mind telling you first after papa and mamma. It *is* true, and there *will* be a marriage in our church some of these days, and you two will be there in new gowns to see your Miss Mary made Mrs. Fitzmuddle."

"Oh, dear, we are so glad," they exclaimed simultaneously. "We do wish you joy with all our hearts, and he such a nice, civil-spoken gentleman, and we thank you so for condescending to tell us; but the house will be awfully dull if you leave it."

"It will be your own fault if you find it dull, Alice," said Mary, "for I shall want a maid after I am married, and I would far rather have an old friend and a Stoke girl, than a stranger; and I would ask Jane too, only I know that she would not be happy away from Stoke while a certain bold baker, Bill Johnson by name, keeps shop there."

Jane tossed her head and said:

"I am sure Bill Johnson is nothing to me, or me to him."

"Fie, fie," said Mary, with a smile, "don't tell stories. I know more than some people suppose. Pray who came to the garden gate two nights ago, and who went to meet him, and whose arm was round whose waist? And if I were put on my oath I could not deny that I heard something that sounded uncommonly like a kiss."

Jane's comely face turned the colour of a peony, and she no longer sought to deny the soft impeachment. So blushing and giggling, the two girls once more wished their mistress joy and retired to the lower regions.

"Oh, how nice, how very nice!" said Alice; "and to think how right you were, Jane, and how the novel has come true! But I know who will be most pleased at the news, and that's Miss Brown; so as I have an errand in the village I'll just put on my bonnet and run down to the school and tell her."

Miss Brown, or to give her full appellation,

Miss Rosa Matilda Brown, was the schoolmistress of the girls' school in the village, and Miss Morton's great ally and trusted aide-de-camp in all matters of charities, Sunday schools, and clothing clubs.   To the outward eye she was a tall, thin, and somewhat angular female of the doubtful age betwen forty and fifty, remarkable chiefly for her staid look, prim attire, a pair of spectacles on her somewhat lengthy nose, and a wonderful and awe-inspiring erection on her head, which might pass for either a castle, a cap, or a bonnet.   But inwardly, she was a good, pious, conscientious Christian woman, with a mind and information superior to her station, and admitted by all to be an excellent schoolmistress.   Her one weak point was a romantic spot left at the bottom of her middle-aged bosom, which made her susceptible to all tender emotions, and the one solace she permitted herself after the duties and labours of the day, was to sit down for half-an-hour with a cup of tea and a yellow-backed novel, and indulge in sentimental tears over the woes of imaginary Belvideras and Clarissas.   She simply idolised Miss Morton; and her mean opinion of the male sex generally was confirmed by the fact that no bold barons and gallant knights came trooping up to the Rectory to do battle for the favour of a glance from her bright eyes.

She was sitting in the school teaching the young idea how to shoot at the mysteries of the multiplication table, when Alice put her head in at the door and said:

"Please, Miss Brown, can you step out and speak to me for just one minute?"

Miss Brown resigned her seat to the eldest pupil and said:

"Now be good girls and stand there quietly for a minute till I come back; and you, Emma Dixon, try to recollect that nine times nine does not make ninety-one. What is it, Alice?" she said. "Nothing wrong, I hope, at the Rectory?"

"Dear me, no," said Alice, "but such delightful news that I knew you would like to hear it before the others. Our Miss Mary is going to be married to the grand, rich gentleman who was carried into the Rectory last month with a broken neck—no, I mean a broken arm; and it's quite true, Miss Mary told Jane and I herself."

"You don't say so!" said Miss Brown; "and what is he like? Is he good enough for our Miss Mary?"

"Well," said Alice, "no one can be quite good enough for her; but he is a real nice, pleasant-spoken gentleman, and I am sure he is as good as gold, and has got a kind heart. You should have seen how he bore the pain of his poor arm and ankle, and never said a word, except to smile and thank us as civilly as if we had been fine ladies, every time Jane or I did the least little thing for him; and they say he is a Right Honourable, which is as good or better than a Lord, and as rich— oh, as rich as rich can be."

Satisfied on this point, Miss Brown gave free reins to her imagination, and pictured all the delights of a real romantic novel of actual life: a wounded hero, a lovely and accomplished heroine, and all going to end with a happy marriage in the village of Stoke, in the county of Duffershire, and the country of England. She conceived a brilliant idea, and going back into the school, said :

" Now, girls, listen to me. I have just heard a piece of joyful news ; our dear, kind Miss Morton is engaged to be married." (Great excitement and shuffling of small feet.) "Now, be quiet a moment, and hear what I have got to say. You shall have a half-holiday, and go out this fine afternoon, and pick all the primroses and violets you can find in the meadows, and we will make wreaths of them, and go up to the Rectory at six o'clock this evening, and present them to her with our best wishes. So be here with your flowers at five sharp ; and now be off with you."

A chorus of little shrill voices at once rose in joyful shout and gleeful giggle, and a stampede was made for the door. In a few minutes the whole little flock were over the stile, and out in the meadows, running for the copse, pushing one another, larking and screaming with delight, and each one anxious to be first to get the best lapful of primroses for their dear Miss Mary.

When six o'clock came, the party in the

drawing-room were aware of a similar, but more subdued, chorus of little voices on the lawn, all talking together, but with a predominant sound of "Miss Mary, Miss Mary," emerging from the confused chatter. It was a fine warm May evening, so they threw up the windows, and stepped out. There stood Miss Brown—emotional, but still majestic—at the head of her little flock, who stepped forward, seized Mary by both hands, and said :

"My dear Miss Mary, we have heard the news, and come to wish you joy; and see what your little pupils have brought you—all these wreaths of their own picking and their own making, just to show you how they love you."

The erection on her head trembled, and so did her voice, as she added :

"But, oh! Miss Mary, how shall we get on without you? You have been like sunshine to us, lightening our dark places."

"How very, very nice and kind of you," said Mary, "and of my dear little children! I do thank you so very much, and I am sure the

Queen never had a nicer present than these beautiful wreaths. I only wish they would keep for ever to remind me of you all, and of dear Stoke. Augustus," she added, "let me introduce you to one of my very best friends— Miss Brown, our excellent schoolmistress; and mind, sir, you have got to like her, if you wish me to like you."

"I won't like her," said Augustus, "I'll love her, for I see she loves you, and I am quite sure from that she must be a most charming and discerning lady."

This speech quite won Miss Brown's heart; she bridled up and smiled, and talking of it next day to her neighbour, Miss Jones, the dressmaker, said :

"If any man could be worthy of our dear Miss Mary—but that's impossible—it would be Mr. Fitzmuddle ; he is such a perfect gentleman."

"And now, Miss Brown, you must come in and have a cup of tea with us," said Mary, "and you, my dears, go into the kitchen. I am sorry there is no cake, for I did not know you were coming, but Jane and Alice will give you a nice thick slice of bread and butter each, and plenty of jam on it."

"And I say," said Augustus, "some day soon, and I hope very soon, if Miss Mary will consent, you shall have a splendid plum cake and an orange each, and as much fruit as you can eat, and a glass of ginger wine each to drink Miss Mary's health and mine, but she won't be Miss then, but Mrs."

A general cheer greeted this announcement, and the flight of little birds took wing to the kitchen, where their tongues were all loosened to tell Jane and Alice what a nice gentleman Miss Mary had got, and they chattered away until their mouths were stopped by the thick hunches of bread with half-an-inch deep of strawberry jam on them.

In the meantime Mary made tea in the drawing-room, and Miss Brown, getting Augustus into a corner, became quite confidential, and was so pleased to talk of Miss Morton's virtues and perfections, and he was so pleased to listen to her, that at last Mary said laughingly: "Why, I declare, Miss Brown, you make me quite jealous; and you, sir, how dare you flirt so outrageously with another lady before my face, and that too on the very day when you seduced me into promising to marry you ? "

Miss Brown simpered and looked pleased, and Augustus vowed that nothing could have taken him for a moment from Mary's side, but the delightful sensation of hearing her praised as she deserved, by a lady of such fine judgment and evident discernment as Miss Brown. And so with the pleasant chaff and simple harmless nonsense that well out from happy hearts, they sat, till the shades of evening gathering in warned Miss Brown that it was time to take her little flock back and dismiss them to their several homes.

When they were gone, Augustus said : "And now, my own dear Mary, those children will be longing for the cake I promised them ; can't you say an early day? There is no earthly reason why we should wait till we are both gray-headed."

"It is too soon to be talking about that," said she, "but now that I have made up my mind to

say 'yes,' I mean to 'love, honour, and obey,' and
you won't find me letting any girlish nonsense
stand in the way of meeting your wishes in any
way I can properly.   And now, Augustus dear,"
she added, "I am going to show that I really
consider myself your property by asking you a
favour."

"How very nice," he said, "to be asked a
favour by you! Three days ago you would not
ask me for a couple of hundred pounds, and I had
to give it on the sly, for fear of offending you."

"I shall never forget that if I live to be a
hundred," said Mary; "but this is not quite a
£200 affair. You saw those dear little girls; I
have taught them in the Sunday school, and I love
them almost as if they were my own children.   I
should so like to have a troop of them for bridesmaids, when we are married in our parish church,
and I want you to agree, and to give a nice white
frock with a rose-coloured sash to half-a-dozen of
the biggest of them.   It would so delight their
little hearts."

"And mine, too, my darling," said he; "it is

the prettiest idea I ever heard of, and I don't
wonder they all love you so, you are so kind and
thoughtful."

"And, Augustus dear," she went on, "there
is just one other thing. You saw what a good old
creature Miss Brown is, would not you like to
make her happy too?"

"Of course I should," said he; "there is
nothing I would not do for her, she spoke so
nicely about you."

"Well," said Mary, "send her a present of a
cream-coloured satin dress made by a fashionable
milliner in London. I know the dear old thing
thoroughly in and out, and I am sure it would
make her happy for the rest of her days. And
how she would talk of it, and how she would
triumph over Miss Jones, and what romances and
castles in the air she would build, whenever she
opened her wardrobe and looked at it! But it
would cost a deal of money, perhaps £15, and I
hardly like to ask you to do it."

"Fifteen pounds!" cried he. "I only wish
it were £150. I am so very glad you thought of

it and told me. But you will choose it, won't you ? I am no great judge of cream-coloured satins ; and while you are about it, you may as well choose some for yourself, so as to lose no time. And I say, Mary, it would be cruel, would it not, to keep Miss Brown and the children waiting a day longer than is necessary ? "

" Perhaps," she said, " but it is a serious matter, and I must take my usual plan of thinking it over and sleeping on it."

CHAPTER XII.

HOW GOLCONDAS WENT UP.

THE result of her deliberations was, that as there was no real reason for postponing the wedding, it was fixed for an early day in autumn. In the meantime, however, the preparations for the important event were considerably facilitated by two strokes of good fortune which befell the sorely-tried finances of the Morton family. In the first place, the affair of the bank turned out, as Mary had predicted, neither quite as well nor quite as badly as they had hoped or feared at the first blush of the intelligence. For a London bank took up the defunct concern, and made arrangements by which depositors could draw out their money, and debtors were not called upon to pay until the securities which they had given arrived at maturity.

But a still greater piece of good fortune befell them, for before the wedding-day arrived, and while the corn was still green, another ray of light beamed on the Rectory from a quarter where the clouds seemed densest, and as in the memorable case of Æneas,

> Via prima Salutis
> Minime quam reres Graia pandetur ab urbe,

Golconda shares actually rose above par.

Thus it occurred. Mr. Sharpus, the shrewd promoter who had brought out the company and put in a board of dummy directors, and appointed the manager in India, and judiciously made him safe by giving him a share of the plunder, was reclining one evening in an easy arm-chair in the bosom of his family, at his well-appointed suburban villa on Sydenham Hill. Now Mrs. Sharpus, though a worthy woman, could hardly be said with truth to be a very entertaining one, so Sharpus yawned and took up a novel which was lying on the table. It chanced to be a novel by a late illustrious statesman, whose loss a whole nation deplored, whether they liked or disliked his politics, and whose enthusiastic admirers have founded a new sect who worship annually at the shrine of St. Primrose. Whig and Tory, Radical and Conservative may well wish that his face, impassive as a marble mask, still looked from the front Conservative bench to rebuke rowdiness and silence vulgarity, and that his voice could be still heard, twanging out short, incisive sentences "like arrows from Apollo's bow," now to raise the spirits of a defeated party, now to stir the heart of a nation to heroic thoughts, but always to show how a gentleman ought to speak in an assembly of gentlemen, and to illustrate by his example the difference between polished invective and coarse scurrility. But to return to Mr. Sharpus and his novel. Amidst a description revelling in oceans of pearls, rivers of rubies, and all the gorgeous upholstery of an Oriental imagination, these words caught his eye, "Golconda diamonds."

To you or me, gentle reader, the reflection which would have occurred would probably have been this : how nice it was to see that this battered and veteran statesman, this hero of a hundred Parliamentary fights, had retained in his extreme old age such an unfeigned, gushing, school-girl admiration for all bright and beautiful things, even if it took the form of Arabian Night-like palaces, and jewels, and marble halls, and velvet carpets, and embroidered draperies!

But Sharpus' reflections were very different. A brilliant idea struck him. How if a hundred pounds or two judiciously invested in South African diamonds, might grow up, like a gourd in the night, into more than as many thousands. As he lay in his bed that night and turned it over, he thought there might be even £10,000 in it. So he rose early, went to his office in Throgmorton Street, and set to work.

The result was that there began to be inquiries for Golconda shares, and a good many odd lots of the £10 shares were picked up quietly at prices ranging from ten shillings to a pound, and rumours began to circulate in the City among the knowing ones, that there was something up in Golcondas. Most thought it was a rig of

Sharpus's, but some believed that gold had really been found, and all concluded that it was safer to buy and trust to getting out on Sharpus's back, than to sell and risk being caught as bears. So the shares kept creeping up. But one day the real rise came, there were buyers for the shares in thousands, and the next day the following paragraph appeared in the financial newspapers:

" EXTRAORDINARY RISE IN GOLCONDA SHARES.—We understand that the rumour of a discovery of diamonds on this Company's property has been fully confirmed, and that a box containing a first instalment of them has been forwarded from India by the manager, and can be seen at the Company's office in Old Jewry."

And then followed some glowing paragraphs bristling with statistics about Kimberley and the South African Mines, and the supply and demand of the diamond-market, and ending by congratulating the possessors of shares on their extraordinary good fortune, and advising immediate purchases, before they went up, as they infallibly would, to a hundred or a thousand per cent. premium.

And so they rose and rose, and went first to par, and then to £5 and then to £10 premium, but the shrewd Sharpus, who remembered the saying that "the public are like the old woman, who, when she began to run, ran very far and very fast," still held on.

Now our dear old Rector, who studied the share-list every day, read all this, but sagely said nothing, for he had a misgiving that, if Mary heard of it, she would make him sell—and Mary had other things to think of than share-lists, until one day she thought she would just take a glance, and see if there was any faint hope of repaying the loan to the bank without selling their furniture. She could hardly believe her eyes when she read :

"Golconda Gold Company Shares, £10 paid —19 to 21, with a buoyant market and large buyers."

She had her father into the library on the instant, and urged immediate sale. He remonstrated for a long while, and declared his con-

viction that they must go to £100. But it is hard
to resist established authority, and Mary had been
so long accustomed to get her own way; and
between ourselves, that authority had been considerably strengthened by her becoming an important personage and being about to marry the
brother of an Earl, with an income of £6,000 a
year.

So she got her way once more, and the Rector
with a sigh gave a reluctant consent, and you may
be sure she put on her bonnet, and ran down to
the post office, and wrote out the telegram herself
to her father's broker, giving the order to sell his
two hundred Golcondas at once, at the best price
he could get.

And the second day after came a letter from
Giles & Co., dated "Drapers' Gardens, Throgmorton Street," to this effect:

"Your telegram received yesterday, too
late for business hours. This was fortunate, for
in the morning there was a fresh rise in Golcondas,
and we sold your two hundred shares at £23.

In the afternoon, prices fell heavily, and there were some ugly rumours afloat, and they closed 15 sellers.

"Your obedient Servants,

"GILES & CO."

And within a week the bubble burst; the ugly rumours were confirmed, for an acute dealer, sharper than Sharpus himself, who had sold a bear at the top price, got a clue, and ran from a cold to a hot scent, and traced the purchase of the South African diamonds, and the passage of a box out to India and back, which bore a marvellous resemblance to the box which came home and was shown at the office, and though Sharpus lied stoutly no one believed him, and— well, he had better have let Mrs. Sharpus talk him to sleep in his arm-chair that evening than have taken up the novel, for he had been dazzled by what seemed the certainty of realising the vision of the £10,000, and held on just a little too long and was caught, and had to dive under for a while, and go to Boulogne for the benefit of his wife's health, who, he suddenly found out, was delicate and wanted sea-air.

And the shares fell and fell, till they relapsed to the original five shillings, and there was great consternation, and meetings of indignant shareholders, and some of them consulted an experienced City man whether they should not prosecute. But his advice was: "On no account. In the first place it is doubtful whether this fellow Sharpus is worth the powder and shot. Then, though the case is morally clear, you never can be sure there is sufficient legal evidence, and what your witnesses may say when the cross-examining thumbscrew of Mr. Serjeant Browbeat, or Mr. Ferret, is brought to bear on them; and moreover, there is one standing axiom which a long experience of commercial matters has impressed upon me, and that is this. If you want to know what the law is in any commercial case, try to reason out what is the common-sense view of the matter, and assume that the direct opposite is probably the law. Acting on this axiom has saved me thousands."

So there was no prosecution, the storm blew over, Mr. Sharpus returned invigorated by the breezes of Boulogne, compounded with his creditors, and went back to his old game of playing (if he could with loaded dice) at the game of contangoes, and backwardations, and premiums, and discounts.

But this solid result remained, that the Rector's debt to the bank was paid off, and his bank-book showed the quite phenomenal balance of £3,600 remaining at his credit. So Mary was not obliged to stint herself in the matter of wedding dresses and presents to her humble dependants, and she would have paid, only Fitzmuddle would not for a single moment hear of such a thing, for that cream-coloured satin which was to make Miss Brown for ever happy.

CHAPTER XIII.

THE WEDDING.

AT length the day arrived, and the wedding came off at the parish church in a style which surpassed the brightest imaginations of Alice and Jane, and afforded matter for gossip for the whole female population of Stoke Regis for years to come, and even to the second generation, a theme for elderly spinsters to descant upon as to the degeneracy of modern times, when such brilliant ceremonies were things of the past.

For the Earl of Muddleton, as beseemed the head of the family, came over with the Countess and two of the little Lady Fitzmuddles, who, after they and the six little village girls in the white frocks and rosy sashes had looked shyly at one another for a few minutes, fraternised, and made a really pretty group of charming little bridesmaids. And the inside of the church was all resplendent with red poppies, and wild corn-flowers, and yellow ears of ripe wheat and barley. And the Bishop came over to assist in the ceremony, which, in the case of distinguished couples, seems to be generally one of such overwhelming difficulty as to overtax the powers of any single ecclesiastic. And the volunteer band from Foxborough came over and discoursed loud, if not eloquent, music. And Alice and Jane were there in their new gowns in a state of rapturous excitement. But above all, Miss Brown towered radiant and majestic in her cream-coloured satin, the envy and admiration of Miss Jones and all the female population of Stoke, with tears gleaming through smiles, like sunbeams through April showers, as her soft heart melted with delight at her dear Mary's marriage, and sorrow· at the thought · of losing her.

The wedding-breakfast was magnificent, with choice flowers, pines, and peaches sent over by the

Earl from Muddleton Hall, and there was no lack of what Tennyson calls

The sparkling wine of Eastern France,

in which the guests drank once and again to the health and happiness of the bride and bridegroom.

Nor were speeches wanting, though it must be confessed that on these occasions they are apt to be a penance to those who have to make them, especially to the bashful young man to whose lot it falls to propose the health of the bridesmaids ; but they have their revenge, for the speeches are apt to be a still greater penance to those who listen to them. However, the wagging of tongues, and the thumping of tables, with cries of " hear, hear," is part of the decent ceremonial of all great occasions where Britons meet, and is, perhaps, a more civilised mode of making a noise than the ancestral method of firing off many guns, and drinking of much ale and whisky.

At least so it appeared on the present occasion, for the Earl's speech, though consisting mainly of a hesitating succession of indifferent jokes, yet heard through the environing atmosphere of his exalted nobility, appeared to the Stoke mind as a bright example of elegant wit and genial affability. And the Bishop's more fluent and sonorous periods, though it must be owned they appeared at the time to be a little long-winded, were long treasured and referred to as a specimen of lofty eloquence. But, after all, the greatest effect was produced by Fitzmuddle himself, for though, as usual, he broke down, and did little more than stammer out a few incoherent sentences about being the luckiest and happiest of men, and his love and affection for Stoke for giving him such a wife as his dear darling Mary, and his fixed determination to do all that he possibly could to show himself in the smallest degree worthy of her ; yet it came from the heart, and what comes straight from one human heart goes straight to others, however imperfect may be the medium by which it is conveyed. Indeed, the less perfect the words the greater often is the effect produced, for the eyes, and expression, and trembling voice, tell of real feeling, while polished sentences show that the speaker is thinking of himself, and what others are thinking of him, instead of being under the sway of genuine emotion.

And as for Mary, she had no need to speak ; you had only to look at her to see all sorts of good and gentle things speaking in her face. For her nature˙was too thorough to do things by halves, and when she had once made up her mind to love, honour, and in all reasonable things obey, she was as incapable of change as the needle of deserting the pole. The little flutterings, and trepidations, and misgivings of weaker natures were altogether unknown to her, and she was calmly and serenely happy, only suffused with a shade of softer emotion when she thought of parting from her parents and home, and from the friends, old and young, whom she saw around her.

Now, reader, although there may be more interest and variety in a more fickle and emotional temperament, believe me, if you have to live your whole life with another person, there is immense comfort in having him or her straightforward and sensible, and being able to rely on finding your companion sure to see things in the right light, and not fret and fidget you by weak indecision, and idle regrets, and misgivings. And if, as the French proverb says, " Le mieux est l'ennemi du bien," it is a comfort not to have your life made miserable by repinings that, although things are well, if they had been done differently they might have been better.

But out-of-doors the enjoyment, if not more real, was decidedly more demonstrative. For two large tables were spread on the lawn, at one of which all the school children of the village were seated, and at the other the old and infirm men and women of the parish. At the juvenile table Fitzmuddle, mindful of his promise on the day of his engagement, had provided a gigantic bride-cake, which towered like a snow-clad mountain above a profusion of smaller cakes, and buns, and tarts, while nearly a waggon-load of fruit of every description had been sent down by train from Covent Garden. Nor were lemonade, gingerbeer, and currant wine wanting, and crackers of brilliant colours and still more brilliant devices. So the little people ate and drank, and stuffed, and chattered, and cheered until you would have thought their young skins must have burst, and their young voices cracked. But young stomachs stand a deal of stuffing, and young throats a deal of straining, and a lot of children are always happy if there is plenty to eat and plenty of noise.

The grave and reverend seniors at the other table were less vociferous, but not the less did they enjoy the noble sirloins of beef, and boiled legs of mutton with turnips, and steaming hot dishes of baked potatoes which graced the board, and not the less valiantly, after having eaten enough of these to last for a fortnight, and washed the whole down with foaming glasses of the best ale, did they attack the gigantic plum puddings which formed the finale of the meal. And the wrinkles in their old withered faces softened out, and their bleared old eyes winked and sparkled as they drained each a goblet of good old port, to drink health and long life to the newly-married couple.

At length the hour of departure came, and as the village of Stoke was too primitive and unsophisticated to have adopted the senseless and inartistic fashionable freak of throwing old shoes and bags of rice, the happy couple drove off amidst a more appropriate shower of flowers, and cheers, and blessings.

END OF VOL. I.

CHARLES DICKENS AND EVANS, CRYSTAL PALACE PRESS.